"Like mother like daughter!"

"She may not have been a very good influence on me with all those marriages, but I'm not *like* her," Veronica bristled.

"Really? I'd heard that you'd got married," Cole accused.

"I did," she replied nervously, knowing what he was getting at.

"And are you still married?"

"No, I'm not married now, but—"

"But you were married," he persisted.

"Yes, I was. But that doesn't mean—"

"Just like your mother, jumping from husband to husband. And now you've come back to the home of one of her husbands.... I don't know what you expect to find here, Veronica."

Susan Fox is an American writer living is Des Moines, Iowa, where she was born. She is married and has two sons, and is happy now to add to her occupation of "housewife" that of author. Her enjoyment in reading romances led to writing them and reflects an early interest in westerns and cowboys. She won a Romance Writers of America Golden Heart Award in 1984 and 1985.

Vows
of the Heart

Susan Fox

Harlequin Books

TORONTO • NEW YORK • LONDON
AMSTERDAM • PARIS • SYDNEY • HAMBURG
STOCKHOLM • ATHENS • TOKYO • MILAN

ISBN 0-373-02763-X

Harlequin Romance first edition May 1986

CHAPTER ONE

VERONICA SPENCER STEERED her rented car into a parking space for the handicapped, grateful to spot a telephone booth nearby. She switched off the engine, then rummaged in her purse for some change, which she then slipped into the pocket of her denim vest.

Slowly, giving her stiff legs a chance to adjust to movement, she opened the door and eased herself out. Once on her feet, she braced a hand on the roof of the car for support while she leaned back in and pulled her crutches from the back seat. She positioned the cushioned pads beneath her arms and let the crutches take a share of her weight before she stepped aside and pushed the door closed.

Veronica glanced around, deciding she found this particular Cheyenne street unaccountably depressing. The faint smile on her soft mouth faded slightly as a gust of warm June wind blew a wisp of brown hair across troubled violet eyes. She was nervous enough about coming here without giving in to some imagined harbinger of doom. Veronica reminded herself that the only problem she was likely to encounter was her stepbrother, Cole Chapman.

Taking the cautiously measured steps she had grown accustomed to, she moved to the sidewalk and headed toward the phone booth. Once inside she closed the door and took out a quarter. In moments the number was dialed, but in a fit of nervousness she hung up the phone before it could ring. The quarter dropped into the coin return, but she let it stay there.

The past six months had been a nightmare of pain and loneliness and rejection. What if Henry Chapman—Hank—the closest she'd ever had to a real father, wasn't glad she'd come to see him? She hadn't spoken to him for several months and he hadn't answered the letters she'd sent.

The reasons she'd given herself for Hank's neglect—he hated writing letters—seemed so flimsy now. Why hadn't she thought of that before she'd traveled more than 1,700 miles?

Veronica forced herself to be calm. Surely her loving all-wise stepfather would have been able to read between the lines and discern how much she needed to see him after all that had happened.

She pressed the coin return and dug out her quarter. Yes, she finally decided, he would have seen her need. She couldn't reconcile callousness with her knowledge of Henry Chapman. After all the years of her mother's neglect and the disruption caused by her several marriages and divorces, only Hank had seen through fourteen-year-old Veronica's adolescent facade of bad behavior. With a little patience and more loving attention than she'd known since her grandmother's death, Hank had transformed her from an obnoxious brat into someone who felt special and lovable.

The man who'd possessed such wonderful qualities of gentleness and understanding wouldn't change toward her. Not now. Her mother's divorce from Hank had wrenched them apart when she'd packed up Veronica and moved to New York. But twice a year Henry Chapman had donned his dress Stetson and city clothes and flown to New York just to see her.

The past year those visits had stopped because of his health. Veronica hadn't made it to Wyoming to see him, but they had kept in touch by phone as regularly as ever. Until six months ago. The last time she had spoken to Hank had been when he'd called to tell her he wouldn't be able to attend her wedding. The heart problem he'd had for years made the trip impossible.

After her wedding and the accident, Veronica hadn't been physically able to call Hank, and after several weeks when she was able, she didn't have the nerve. Then, a couple of months ago when she finally started to climb out of the mire of self-pity, she wrote to him. A few days later she realized that a visit to the wisest and kindest man she'd ever known might help her pick up the pieces of her shattered existence. And now she was here.

Veronica dropped the coin into the slot and dialed again. This time, she let it ring.

COLE CHAPMAN LEANED BACK in the heavy swivel chair behind his desk and ran a tanned thickly callused hand through black hair overdue for a trim. The handsome arrangement of his facial features bore the sun-browned stamp of an outdoorsman, the fine wrinkles that fanned out from cobalt-blue eyes evidence of squinting into the sun. Deep grooves on each side of the grim set of his mouth hinted at happier times. As he reached back to massage stiff neck muscles, his eyes automatically sought the digital readout of the clock on his desk. It was half past eleven, but the time didn't register as his gaze slid to the photograph of his wife.

As happened at odd times, Cole felt a fresh pang of heartache. Four years after the fatal brain aneurism that had wrenched her so permanently from his arms, he still mourned his wife, Jacqueline. So beautiful, so cheerful, so full of life, so...perfect. Suddenly impatient with himself, Cole's gaze veered to the other eight by ten inch wooden frame on his desk. As always, the picture of their son, Curtis, comforted him, swelling his heart with gratitude that Jackie had left him with a child.

The phone on the corner of the desk rang stridently in the silent room. Irritably he reached for the receiver.

"CHAPMAN RANCH."

Veronica shivered. Some things never changed. Cole Chapman's gruff voice sounded just as harsh as ever.

"Cole?" She hated the timidity in her voice, but she had long ago lost the ability to sound self-assured.

"Yes. Who's this?"

"It's Veronica." When she spoke this time, it was with a bit more confidence.

"Veronica who?" There was a long silence as Veronica tried to harden herself to her stepbrother's relentless dislike.

"Veronica Spencer."

A low sarcastic chuckle came across the line.

"So, the bad penny finally shows up. Did you decide to cash in on your gold mine?" Again he made the mirthless sound while Veronica puzzled over his remark. "I think you've waited long enough to prove to everyone you aren't the little mercenary your mother is. To everyone but me, however."

Veronica swallowed hard at the insult, but didn't respond in kind. She had no idea what Cole was talking about and no desire to get into an argument.

"I'm not interested in your money. I'm in Cheyenne and I want to see your father." Veronica clutched the phone nervously as silence stretched for several heart-beats.

"I suppose it's better late than never," Cole finally answered. "You know where you can find him."

"No, I don't know," she responded with brittle patience. "Perhaps you wouldn't mind giving me a clue. You know I haven't been home...er here, for several years."

"It's too bad you didn't stay away."

Veronica pressed a trembling hand to her forehead as she tried to hold back the resurgence of unhappy memories.

"Please, Cole," she urged. "I know how you feel about me, but I just came to see your father." Tears welled in her eyes as she waited, wondering how she could have forgotten the depth of her stepbrother's hatred.

"You remember which cemetery my mother is buried in, don't you?"

"Yes."

"That's where you'll find him."

The line went dead and Veronica hung up the phone. Of course, she remembered. Hank had taken her there several times. He frequently made short visits to Margaret Chapman's grave, making certain it was kept up.

Knowing she had to hurry or risk missing Hank, Veronica turned to leave the booth. Above all, she wouldn't go to the ranch unless Hank invited her. And when he did, Cole would have nothing to say about it.

AN HOUR LATER, the black desk phone at the Chapman Ranch rang again. Irritated by the thought it might be Ronnie calling back, Cole grabbed the receiver and snapped out a hello.

"Cole?" The feminine voice at the other end of the connection was like Veronica's, but it wasn't. It was a voice that hadn't changed in eight years.

"What do you want, Miriam?" Cole asked curtly.

"Has Veronica contacted you yet?" The older woman's voice sounded anxious.

"As a matter of fact, she did call. About an hour ago."

"What did you tell her?"

"I made it plain she isn't welcome here. The same goes for you." Cole had never liked his father's second wife. After Miriam left his father for a younger richer man, he had liked her even less, although he'd always counted it a blessing that she had taken her delinquent daughter back east with her.

"Please listen to me, Cole." The feminine voice hesitated. "Veronica doesn't know about your father's death."

"What do you mean she doesn't know?" Cole's stern face went tight with anger. What were the two of them pulling?

"She doesn't know, Cole. It's a long complicated story."

"Then shorten it," he ordered impatiently. "I've got work to do."

"Oh, Cole." Miriam's voice trailed away into a seizure of sniffles and Cole muttered a curse. "About six months ago," the woman went on at last, "just the day before your father died, Veronica was involved in a very serious automobile accident." Miriam was nearly sobbing now. "We-we didn't know for days if she'd even live, and when she did, she had so many problems that I couldn't bear—"

"When were you planning on telling her?" Cole broke in, provoked by Miriam's everlasting irresponsibility.

"She's had so many disappointments," Miriam wailed.

"And she probably deserves every one of them." Cole felt almost no sympathy for either Miriam or her daughter. "She can console herself with her share of the ranch." As much as he'd loved his father, it still galled him that Hank had willed Ronnie a one-quarter interest.

"She's been hurt so badly," Miriam blubbered on. "She can barely walk."

It took a few seconds for the nearly incoherent words to sink in. Cole's first thought was that Miriam was exaggerating.

"Veronica's only been out of the rehabilitation center a few days," she continued. "I don't know where she got this foolish idea. I just came home and she was gone. Oh, Cole!" Miriam's voice was pleading and Cole felt his conscience being prodded.

"Give me your phone number, Miriam," he growled, hating that he suddenly felt obligated to become involved. He scrawled the hastily given area code and number on a note pad. "I'll see what I can do."

"Thank you, Cole, thank you—"

Cole dropped the phone into the cradle, torn between his anger at the mother and a reluctant twinge of compassion for the daughter.

VERONICA MOVED with care but unavoidable awkwardness, the trembling in her weak legs making her even more unsteady. She was grateful for a distraction from her grief while the owner of the motel carried her luggage into a room. She handed him a small bill and watched as he left and pulled the door closed behind him.

She couldn't cry yet. Not even the vivid memory of what she'd seen after her labor up the grassy incline to

Margaret Chapman's grave released the tears. How long had she stood before the double headstone and stared at the date of death beneath Henry Chapman's name. An hour?

Veronica moved tiredly to the drawer unit along the wall and methodically unwrapped a glass from its sanitary wrapper. Her only stop between the cemetery and this motel had been a liquor store. Thanks to the man who'd carried her things from the car, the bottle of whiskey she'd purchased sat within reach along with the can of cola she'd bought from a machine in the motel office.

Veronica seemed incapable of more than fragments of thought. Her whole being was engulfed by the grief she felt for a man everyone else had mourned months ago. She hadn't made a conscious connection between the date of Hank's death and the date of her own tragedy, yet her mind was reeling with a hundred questions she couldn't seem to concentrate on. All she knew was that the person she had needed to see for so long was gone. When Hank Chapman was alive, Veronica had always felt she had someone to come back to, a home, love. Now she was truly adrift. She was both saddened and terrified.

Veronica remembered the whiskey she'd bought. She reached for the bottle, and with fingers that trembled twisted open the cap and splashed a too-generous amount of the amber liquid into the glass. Forgetting to add the cola, she raised her hand and forced herself to take the first sickening gulp, choking on the stinging bite that followed. She was not normally a drinker, but she needed desperately to dull the awful feeling that nothing good would ever happen in her life again.

COLE WALKED QUICKLY down the sidewalk that skirted the motel. He'd already checked out five other motels, but it was this one that had a Veronica Spencer registered. According to the clerk, she'd been there for more than two hours. Cole had made a late start from the ranch, and when he found out she'd already left the cemetery he assumed she'd be at the airport. More time had been wasted there and still more while he and one of his men made the round of motels.

When Cole reached number eight, he knocked. There was no sound from inside and no answer to his second knock. He turned the door knob on the off chance it wasn't locked, and the door swung inward. Stepping into the dimness, he waited for his eyes to adjust from the bright afternoon sunlight before he pushed the door closed, his blue gaze already fixed on the prone figure on the bed.

As Cole crossed the room, uncertainty ripped through him. The girl lay nearly face down across the bed. A half-empty bottle and tumbled glass were on the floor below fingers that hung limply over the edge of the mattress. He wondered if there had been a mixup in the room number.

The shoulder-length hair was the same mink brown as the waist-length tresses Ronnie had worn as an adolescent, but he could not be sure it was her. Miriam had warned him that Ronnie was changed, and the pair of crutches propped against the chair were what he'd been led to expect. But as he looked down at the frail, too-thin body on the bed, it amazed him to think this was Veronica.

Cole crouched low and gently brushed aside the smooth thick strands of hair that obscured the girl's face. Black streaks of mascara stained the unhealthy pallor of her cheeks, and her puffy reddened eyes were smudged with what remained of a bluish eye shadow.

Cole was astonished. It was Veronica, but her face was a pale echo of the glowing natural beauty he remembered. Carefully he eased her onto her back and straightened her legs. She weighed almost nothing. Cole sat on the bed by her hip and automatically reached for her wrist to take her pulse. It was steady, but for a fraction of a second he'd feared the worst.

Cole sat there for several moments more, staring at the physical changes eight years had wrought. He resisted the idea that Ronnie was any different from the spoiled, grasping little delinquent she had been. His dislike for her was still too intense for him to believe that.

A wave of compassion rushed at the wall of rock that was his heart. The thought of taking Ronnie to the ranch for a few days to give her time to get over the shock entered his mind. He wouldn't have sent her to that cemetery if he'd had any idea she'd never been told of his father's death. For that he was truly sorry.

But then common sense warned he would be letting himself in for endless problems if he did take her home. He had Curtis, his seven-year-old son, to consider. Helen, his sister-in-law, looked after Curtis in her home on the neighboring ranch during the day and would probably be willing to keep him round the clock for two or three days. But did he want all their lives disrupted for Veronica? As long as she was at the ranch, he would have to give up precious time with his son. What kind of problems would he have with Ronnie? She did have a quarter interest in the ranch. What if she suddenly decided she wanted to stay and oversee that interest?

Cole's lips thinned unpleasantly. If Miriam had had any backbone at all, she would have told Veronica about

Hank's death months earlier and spared them all this. But as usual Miriam had thought of little more than making things easy on herself.

Now Cole felt he was being saddled with the same problem his father had, more than ten years before. Hank had taken the impossible little Veronica on and had tried to give her the love and discipline her mother had been incapable of giving her. And not once had Hank voiced any regret. Cole had never understood that or the fact that his father had continued to think of Ronnie as a daughter, even after Miriam had divorced him and re-married.

Veronica's head moved slightly on the pillow and a small moan of pain came from her lips. Her breathing had changed and Cole started to shake her gently, but she was too deeply asleep. He picked up the half-consumed bottle and examined it with faint disgust. It would be hours before she slept it off.

Cole got up and walked into the bathroom. Taking a washcloth from the towel bar, he moistened it beneath the warm-water faucet before he returned to her bedside. As gently as possible, he wiped away the dark smudges of eye makeup, then studied the pale face he'd uncovered. Suddenly he pitched the washcloth across the room in anger.

He didn't want the responsibility of Veronica Spencer. He didn't want to know her problems and he didn't want her intruding on his life. But his father's will made that unavoidable. Still, it was Cole who made the decisions around the ranch now. Veronica may have a quarter interest, but when he decided she would leave, she'd damned well clear out.

WHEN VERONICA AWOKE, it was dark. She felt ill and it was all she could do to roll to the edge of the bed. She was too sick to be startled by the barrier that stopped her before she could get one foot on the floor. Her only thought was that someone had left her hospital bed rail up. Frantically she tried to find the button to summon a nurse as she fought down a tide of nausea.

"Are you going to be sick?" asked a deep rough voice. Veronica panted her reply and was immediately pulled from the bed and carried through the darkness.

The suddenness of the bright bathroom light brought a searing pain to her head. Strong arms lowered her to her knees and held her steady over the bowl. Again and again the sickness came until she was limp and the nausea spent. Veronica heard the faucet being twisted on behind her and the rush of water that followed.

The cool wet cloth that was forced into her fingers was soothing as she ran it over her face. She already felt worlds better. She didn't resist when the cloth was taken impatiently from her fingers and held beneath the cold water again. This time, the cloth was guided over her face by a surer hand than her own.

"Here." The cloth was removed and a glass of water held in front of her. "Rinse your mouth." She should have known immediately whose voice was giving the orders, but her brain was still muddled. She obeyed. The glass was taken away and the room grew still. Veronica was weak and tired but her mind was beginning to clear. She knew now who had held her steady and witnessed her sickness. She knew and was recovered enough to feel deeply ashamed.

"Thank you, Cole," she got out, wondering why he was at her motel. She was just about to ask when it dawned on her that this was her old bathroom at the ranch. "How did I get here?" She'd heard of alcoholic blackouts and was suddenly terrified she'd just had one.

"I brought you here," was the gruff reply. The note of regret in Cole's deep voice was easily detected.

"I'm sorry." She must have said that to him hundreds of times in the more than two years she'd lived here, but Cole Chapman rarely accepted her apologies. "I need to be alone in here for a few minutes," she told him quietly.

"Can you manage by yourself?" There was no concern in his voice. It was simply a question he needed to ask. Veronica nodded and was lifted to her feet. Cole was out of the bathroom and had closed the door behind him before she realized she hadn't actually seen him yet.

Veronica moved carefully into the bedroom, using the wall to steady herself. The bright bathroom light had been painful, but the soft light from the lamp Cole had left on beside the bed was soothing. Her gaze wandered lovingly around the room that had changed little in eight years.

It was still decorated in spring green and white, from the tiny white flowers and vines on the puffed green comforter to the white ruffled curtains with green tiebacks. The dark luster of woodwork accented the wallpaper, which was a reverse of the comforter, with green flowers and vines on a white background. She remembered the horrified reaction her mother'd had when she chose this color scheme the first month they lived on the ranch. Veronica's lips moved into a wry line. Her taste and her mother's had always clashed.

Being in this house again, this room, brought back a lot of memories. For a brief moment, Veronica was lost in the odd sensation that she'd never really left, that the eight years she'd been away had somehow been compressed into days.

But Hank wasn't here now. Remembering that brought a crush of grief so strong it forced the air from her lungs in a rush. Wearily she lowered herself onto the straight chair next to the bathroom door.

Cole watched from the hallway, reluctant to intrude. Ronnie's too-thin shoulders shook with mute sobs and her head was bowed dejectedly. He wasn't prepared for the sudden rush of compassion he felt at the sight of her grief. It reached for him, tore into the still-tender areas of his own heart. His first step toward her was hesitant.

Veronica heard Cole's soft footfalls and went rigid. She straightened self-consciously and smeared the wetness from her cheeks. She noticed then that her watch and jewelry had been removed.

"What time is it?" she asked quietly, trying unsuccessfully to hide her misery from her stepbrother.

"Midnight."

Veronica looked up at Cole for the first time. Eight years had seasoned his smooth dark handsomeness into a more appealingly rugged look. The sun had defined the lines that fanned out from dark blue eyes, while the slashing grooves on each side of his mouth boldly accented the sensuality of his firm lips. His jaw was still the strong implacable jaw she recalled, but it was rough now with whisker stubble. He was as lean and hard as ever, his body the body of an athlete, wide shouldered, narrow hipped....

Veronica's eyes shied away. She would never let Cole see her make more than a cursory assessment. She'd had a crush on him once and had been foolish enough to confess her love to him. After that, Cole rarely had anything good to say to her or about her. Those were the memories that hurt.

"H-how did Hank die?" Veronica asked, bracing herself for the answer.

"He had a heart attack," Cole began quietly. "We rushed him to the hospital, but after they got him into intensive care, he had another one and they couldn't revive him."

The huskiness in Cole's voice made her feel close to him; they had both loved Hank Chapman deeply. But after a few silent moments Veronica raised damp eyes darkening with resentment to meet the watchful depths of her stepbrother's.

"Why didn't you notify us? You knew how much I—" She bit her lip, not wanting Cole to see her cry. "And you sent me to his grave knowing what a shock it would be." Veronica's pale features flushed with the effort it took to restrain her tears. She trembled with anger, but the hurt she felt was overwhelming. Cole crossed the small space between them, then crouched down in front of her.

"I did notify your mother. She wasn't home when I called the first time, but one of her servants took the message. When I called later that day, she was still out, but her husband assured me Miriam had already been informed." Cole paused and reached out to touch the small white hand that rested on her thigh. "I wouldn't have kept my father's death a secret, Ronnie, no matter how much hostility there was between us."

The solemn expression she saw on Cole's face blurred as tears surged into her eyes. "I don't believe you," she whispered desolately. "You always resented that Hank treated me like—" Like a daughter, her heart finished for her. Cole's fingers tightened gently around hers.

"Miriam called just after you did today and she admitted she hadn't told you about Hank." Cole let Ronnie's statement pass. Maybe he had resented how quickly Ronnie and his father had taken to each other. He'd certainly never understood why.

Ronnie shook her head. "Six months? For six months she kept it from me?" Veronica was incredulous. Cole's lips twisted sarcastically.

"Miriam outdid herself this time."

Veronica threw off Cole's consoling hand.

"Don't you dare criticize her! My mother was never as bad as you always said. And you don't know anything about her now."

Cole stared. Ronnie was overwrought and surely not rational. Where was the resentment she'd always borne Miriam? Miriam had never inspired any kind of loyalty in her daughter and now she was defending her?

"Where are my car keys?" She had to get out of there. The restless sense of panic she felt demanded she do something.

"They're in my pocket," Cole answered. "You won't be going anywhere tonight." Veronica opened her mouth to protest, but Cole interrupted. "You're in no shape to be driving."

"I'm sober," she told him angrily.

"I know you are, but you aren't well." Cole stood. It was then that she noticed the row of luggage he must have carried in earlier. "Which case has your nightgown?"

Veronica didn't answer right away as she watched Cole cross to her bags, select one at random, then open it. "The small one," she was forced to say before he began rummaging on his own. Cole snapped the larger piece shut and reached for the case she'd indicated. Opening it, he also retrieved her toiletry and cosmetic bag.

In moments he'd draped her nightgown and robe across the foot of the bed. Then, he carried her cosmetic case into the bathroom and placed most of its contents on the wide counter that skirted the sink. When he finished he came back into the room and handed her the crutches.

"You'll have to dress yourself." Cole walked to the head of the bed and turned down the comforter and sheet before pushing the chair he had used earlier back into the corner.

Cole's take-charge activity had a settling effect on Veronica's nerves. She was exhausted and the inviting sight of clean sheets and a comfortable bed made her ache to lie down.

Her murmured thank-you carried a note of unconscious submission. Cole's impersonal gaze swept over her as she rose shakily from the chair.

"Sleep in as long as you need to. If you miss breakfast, there should be enough food in the refrigerator for you to help yourself."

Ronnie murmured another thanks and Cole moved toward her. She sensed his uncertainty, his reluctance, when he stopped bare inches from her. In the next moment, he wrapped her in his arms, pressing her firmly against his warm chest. Veronica stiffened. She knew that Cole's comfort was solely an observance, a hollow gesture of commiseration. The dutifully performed amenity cut her to the quick, astonishing her with the realization that she wanted much more from him than a dutiful embrace. Awkwardly she drew away and Cole released her as if he couldn't bear to touch her any longer.

"I'll be on my way as soon as possible in the morning," she told him as she grasped the crutches and moved past him to the foot of the bed.

"There's no hurry," he said, a little surprised at his almost welcoming response.

"Isn't there?" She wanted to demand why he'd brought her to the ranch in the first place. She didn't have the physical or emotional strength to deal with both Hank's death and the problems of dragging herself and her belongings from place to place. Why hadn't Cole just left her at the motel?

"As long as you're here you might as well stay a couple of days. There are a few things we need to discuss. The sooner we have our talk, the better."

"What do we have to talk about?" Veronica reached for her nightgown, hoping Cole would just leave. Now that Hank was gone there was no one to mediate their quarrels. Veronica was not about to get into any discussions with Cole.

"You'd be surprised, Ronnie. Good night."

Veronica listened to Cole's booted stride cross the green rug, then heard the soft click of the door as he closed it behind him.

"Good night, Cole," she whispered.

VERONICA SLEPT DEEPLY, then woke to the strangeness of a new environment just after five A.M. Fixing bleary eyes on the small travel alarm on the nightstand, she decided it had been the muffled sounds of activity at the other end of the house that had awakened her. Her head pulsed with pain, but she managed the short trip from bed to bathroom to take some aspirin and have a shower.

Rapidly, with a skill born of necessity, Veronica cleaned her face in preparation for the foundation makeup that preceded the special combination of shadings, blushers and eye shadow she used to artfully conceal her pallor. She believed this restored some part of the beauty she felt she'd lost since the accident. When she finished drying her hair, she scooped up her makeup and toiletries and put them in their case.

It took little time to pack. Making the bed was a challenge, but when she finished, the room bore no traces of her presence other than the luggage lined up by the door and the white slacks and pink blouse she'd taken out to wear. With luck, she would be on her way to the Cheyenne airport within an hour. She quickly dressed and went to the kitchen.

Savoring the delicious aroma of bacon and freshly brewed coffee, Veronica gingerly lowered herself onto a chair at the only place at the table not already set for breakfast. She watched Cole's uncommunicative back with some trepidation. Upon her entrance into the big kitchen, Cole had tossed a barely civil good-morning over his shoulder while he continued his work at the stove.

Veronica knew better than to ask Cole why he was doing the cooking, drearily remembering that he had little patience for questions before six A.M., especially hers. For now she allowed herself a few quiet moments to look around the big kitchen, marveling again how little the Chapman ranch house had changed in eight years.

The spacious living room she'd just come through was much the same, but the traditional furnishings, which had seen better days, were now arranged more for convenience than aesthetics. Her mother had tried to make inroads into Hank's uncaring attitude toward interior decoration, but he had resisted most of the major changes. Apparently Cole's wife had not had the time or inclination to make many alterations, either.

The kitchen remained relatively unchanged, too, although a dishwasher had been installed under one section of the counter and a big microwave oven rested beneath one of the cupboards. It was amazing how much work and storage space the kitchen had. With cupboards and counters taking up nearly three walls, the room was ideal for preparing large meals for the men who worked at the ranch.

The clatter of a plastic bowl falling to the floor then wobbling hollowly in a circle drew Veronica's attention back to Cole. As he bent to retrieve it he suddenly seemed to be reminded of her presence and he scowled darkly at her. Snatching up the bowl, he turned away to toss it into the sink and get another one from the cupboard.

The grief she'd somehow managed to put aside temporarily suddenly overwhelmed her under Cole's sharp look. It was a look that seemed to blame her presence for the small calamity, and when he turned back to the stove to fish more bacon from the hot grease, Veronica rose stiffly to make a silent retreat.

Once in her room, she stretched out across the bed and lay quietly. When she heard the sound of the voices of Cole's men coming in for breakfast, she was relieved she'd fled the kitchen. She wondered if she'd know any of them now and strained to hear a familiar voice.

The good-natured ribbing Cole was getting brought a faint smile to her lips. She could hear his men bemoaning the fact that the boss still hadn't found a cook, and the complaints ranged from burnt bacon to rubbery scrambled eggs. Even Cole's not-so-good-natured reply that the next one who complained had to cook the next meal didn't subdue them, their laughter and joking continued until they evidently started to eat.

The sounds emanating from the kitchen reminded Veronica of her happier days on Chapman Ranch. But after a few moments tears again streaked from the corners of her eyes and into her hair, as she grieved for Hank and the simple happy life-style he'd once shared with her. In her two years at the ranch, she'd been Hank's shadow, eager to go anywhere with him. Whether she was helping with the spring roundup and the endless summer work that followed, or braving the frigid temperatures and deep snowfalls of winter to get hay to the cattle, or helping in the calving sheds, she'd done it all, loved it all, because she was with Hank.

A new wave of sadness engulfed her as she was reminded that those times were as lost to her as Hank—the man who'd given her pleasant memories of a childhood place beyond the home her grandmother had made for her until she was six years old. In all her growing-up years since her grandmother's death, the Chapman ranch had been the only place where someone had really cared for her.

The simple well-ordered life-style in which she'd received the guidance, discipline and affection she'd needed had had a profound effect on the young teenager, whose insolent behavior had been an unconscious ploy to force her mother to notice her. Hank had been the only one of her mother's husbands Veronica hadn't been jealous of. He was also the only one who didn't regard her as a nuisance who needed to be put in a boarding school and farmed out to camp for the summer.

A sharp rap sounded at her door and Veronica hastily reached for a tissue from the night table.

"Veronica?"

She struggled awkwardly to sit up and move to the edge of the bed. She wasn't ready for Cole. Not yet. She'd realized that in the kitchen. Veronica couldn't take his harshness and miserably wondered if she'd be able to take any sign of gentleness either. She was terrified at the thought of turning into a pathetic blubbering fool if Cole said the wrong thing to her, and her face went white with the effort it took to lock herself into tight control.

"Come in." She wiped away the last of the wetness and forced the hurt to subside as Cole opened the door. To her surprise Cole was carrying a big tray laden with two steaming plates of food. He entered briskly and set the tray on the desk near the window, then headed back to the hall. When he returned he brought another tray with a large glass of milk and juice and coffee for them both.

Veronica remained sitting on the edge of the bed while Cole cleared the desk and arranged their plates. It surprised her that he was going to so much trouble, but she was secretly thrilled that he obviously intended to eat with her. For the past six months her solitary hospital meals had been her least favorite time of the day, and so sharing a meal with anyone was a welcome treat.

"It might not be the best breakfast you've ever had, Veronica, but it's nourishing and hot." Cole was looking at her now, and at the prompting lift of his dark brows, she reached for her crutches and got to her feet. Iron-faced, Cole waited until she was seated before he sat down.

"I couldn't remember if you liked your eggs scrambled or fried," Cole began as she picked up her fork. The mere suggestion of a smile appeared at his mouth as one corner lifted fractionally. "Of course, no matter how they start out, they always manage to end up that way."

A small smile altered the set of Veronica's own mouth. "Most people don't realize how difficult it is to cook eggs properly, so don't apologize," she said, then dug into the leaden-looking curds of scrambled egg, determined to eat every bite. She never would have expected Cole to be so thoughtful and hoped in some small way that her pleasant remark had rewarded his gesture.

A quick glance at his plate revealed that her eggs looked more appetizing than the ones he'd served himself. Also, the hash browns on her plate appeared more uniformly cooked and the bacon a little less crisp. That he'd provided her with the better plate of food touched her.

Yet the meal passed tensely. Veronica sensed that Cole was avoiding mention of Hank, and she barely spoke at all, uncertain of this man who'd been such a reluctant stepbrother all those years before.

When Cole's gaze drifted toward the window, she glanced at him covertly and let her eyes wander slowly over his tanned face. To her consternation, the growing light from the sunrise accentuated the small scar that interrupted the well-shaped line of his nose just below its bridge—a permanent reminder of the time she'd accidentally whacked him with a pitchfork handle. Reminded of one trespass, she automatically recalled others.

Her memories of Hank were wonderful, but the memories associated with Cole were tormenting. In her two years at the ranch she had managed to provoke Cole at every turn, earning his hostility when she secretly craved his acceptance and affection.

Her eyes started to fill with tears again and she set her fork down a bit too firmly. Cole's attention had returned to her, and her lips quirked sheepishly as she used her napkin to blot the wetness from beneath her eyelashes. To her relief, he made no comment and soon they were both eating again. By the time she finished the last of the glass of milk Cole was leaning back with his coffee.

"Thank you for breakfast, Cole." She reached for her coffee and tasted it. "I certainly didn't expect you to go to the trouble of bringing it in to me." She paused to take a nervous breath. "And thank you for joining me." Her eyes shied away from his, then warily wavered back. She felt as unsure and intimidated by him as ever, but to her immediate relief, Cole allowed himself a neutral smile.

"I notice you've packed your things. I thought we'd agreed that you would stay on a couple of days." Cole's voice was low, almost gentle, arrowing straight into her vulnerable heart. He was watching her intently now. She felt her cheeks flush and was unable to voice the polite refusal she wanted to make. Perhaps Cole was making this gesture because it was something he felt obligated to do, or maybe he still felt guilty about sending her to the cemetery. Whatever the reason, she knew that if he had a preference, it would be for her to leave.

"I can't," she finally got out, then set her coffee aside.

Cole leaned back in his chair and raised a booted foot to rest on his thigh. "My father made a bequest to you in his will, Ronnie, and it's something you and I need to discuss. Since you're here, I'd just as soon get it settled before you leave."

Veronica's eyes widened in shock at this news. Hank had left her something in his will? She felt the weight in her heart grow heavier as she thought about what Cole's reaction to that must have been. *Did you decide to cash in on your gold mine?*

"I'm sorry, Cole." Veronica flinched inwardly at the oft-repeated phrase. "I had no idea. Of course, I'll refuse to accept it, whatever it is."

"You don't even know what you've inherited." The irritation in his voice increased her unease and she fidgeted with her napkin.

"All right," she conceded quietly. "What have I inherited?"

"My father willed you a one-quarter interest of everything he owned. That includes not only the ranch, but the Montana mining interests his brother left him years ago."

Veronica shook her head slightly, unable for a moment to grasp the meaning of his words. She had expected perhaps a few thousand dollars at the most, but a one-quarter interest? Hank had never been one to flaunt his wealth, preferring a much simpler life than he could actually afford, but she was certain that because of the mining interests Hank had been a millionaire. Veronica reached for her crutches and stood wordlessly.

Finally, she managed to collect her thoughts. "Your father was always generous with his time and affection." Her voice wavered precariously on the last word. "But his money and his property really belong to you and your son." Veronica's shoulders straightened. "If you'll give me the name of your lawyer, I'll see him before I leave today and have him draw up whatever papers are necessary to see that it's all returned to you."

Veronica turned away, overwhelmed by the significance of the inheritance. A man her mother had been married to for only two years and then betrayed had not only provided her with her childhood ideal of a father, but had also left her a part of what rightfully belonged exclusively to his natural son.

Warm steady hands closed over her slim shoulders, preventing her from moving away.

"As much as I would benefit from letting you do that, Ronnie, I wouldn't feel right about taking it. I'd planned to make you an offer." Cole's thumbs began to move in slow warm circles that sent a new kind of shock through her system as she felt an answering heat pulse to life in her veins. Panicked by the sensation, Veronica shrugged off his grip, stepping away to a safe distance.

"I think I'm a little confused by all this," she said. "It's all happening so fast." She managed a thin smile as she hazarded a sideward glance. "Would you mind giving me an hour or two to pull myself together?" She was close to tears again, unable to find the strength to keep her emotions under control for very long.

"I've already offered you a couple of days, Ronnie—more if you need them." Cole's voice was gruff but not unkind.

"I know that, but I don't think I should stay." The sound she made was intended as a short laugh, but came out grimmer than she'd intended. "If I did, it wouldn't be long before I'd manage to get on your wrong side and we'd have a fight."

Cole's brow darkened ominously.

"Don't you see?" she whispered sadly. "It's happening already."

"Well, dammit, let it happen. We're both adults now and surely we can work out our differences." Cole stopped, then sighed, running a tanned hand through his thick black hair. "I'm sorry, Veronica. That came out harsher than I intended. Why don't you rest awhile, then come on into the study when you feel up to it. I'll get finished up in the kitchen and we can talk later." Cole waited for her to respond and at last, resigned, she nodded her agreement.

She had been caught off guard by Cole's apology. True, his regretting his harshness had been a small thing, but any kind of apology from Cole was a step out of the old pattern between them.

"I think I might rest awhile, then."

"Take all the time you need. If you sleep through lunch you won't starve." The smile Cole suddenly gave her struck her emotions with the impact of a runaway freight train.

She had seen Cole charm countless other women with that smile. At sixteen she would have eagerly given her life for the privilege of being the recipient of a fraction of the charm he'd lavished on other females.

Now at twenty-four she could appreciate the irony of finally having an adolescent wish fulfilled—but only after Cole Chapman was more romantically inaccessible to her than ever.

CHAPTER TWO

VERONICA RETURNED THE PHONE to its cradle, relieved that the emotionally charged conversation with her mother was over. Miriam had been tearfully contrite about keeping Hank's death a secret, and then adamant in her appeal—no, her insistence—that Veronica return to New York as soon as possible.

Veronica leaned back comfortably in Cole's big swivel chair, a warm feeling of security enveloping her. For most of her life, she had been Miriam's little complication. In these past few months, however, the scatterbrained social butterfly who loved to play the role of enchantress seemed to have vanished, and in her place, a remarkably sensitive and compassionate parent had evolved, fretting over her only child, pampering her, loving her. When Eric, Veronica's husband, decided after the accident that he'd chained himself to a bride who was suddenly less than the physical perfection his vanity required, Miriam had consoled her, devoting hours on end to her daughter in a campaign to coax Veronica from life-threatening depression.

It had taken Veronica weeks to recover emotionally from Eric's abandonment. It was little wonder her mother had avoided adding a new shock just as Veronica had begun to cooperate with the professionals who were working to restore the use of her legs.

Too bad, Veronica mused, that Charles Whitcomb, her most recent stepfather, regarded the situation between mother and daughter with barely concealed impatience. He was the reason Veronica was in no hurry to return to New York. As much as she loved her mother now and treasured their new relationship, she didn't want to be the cause of Miriam's sacrificing the only marriage she'd ever found contentment in. Veronica hadn't made any definite plans for the future, but she was certain she had to find some gentle way of redirecting her mother's attention from her and her problems to the husband who had so jealously awaited his stepdaughter's recovery. What she needed now was some excuse to delay her return to New York. Perhaps she could do a bit of traveling, résumé in hand, or visit a few of her friends....

Her brief sense of security evaporated. It was time to come to a decision about her future. Now that she was well out of college, single once again and unemployed, she needed to make some definite plans. Veronica knew that coming back to Hank and this ranch had been an effort to delay making the decision.

The splintering crash of glassware made an almost welcome intrusion into the unpleasant turn her thoughts had taken. By the time she got to the kitchen Cole was wiping slivered pieces of glass from the sink and shaking the dishcloth of fragments over the trash can. It was obvious from the haphazard assembly of tableware and food that he was beginning preparations for the noon meal.

"Is there anything I can help you with?" she offered hesitantly, unable to tell from Cole's granite profile whether he would tolerate her presence or not.

"Not unless you learned to cook somewhere along the line." Cole dropped the dishcloth into the trash can, then turned on the taps to rinse any unseen bits of glass down the drain. When he finished and returned the trash can to its customary place at the end of the counter, he turned back to her. The cynical look in his eyes told her he doubted she'd be much help. After all her mother had been nearly useless in the kitchen.

"Cooking is one of my favorite hobbies. It's something I'm good at." Veronica felt color seep into her cheeks at her impulsive boast, then chagrin when his dark brows rose in exaggerated amusement. She didn't add that she had minored in food and nutrition at college.

Instead she felt awkward and embarrassed, certain he would decline her offer. "Of course, I haven't had much practice these past months." Now her mind was darting frantically, trying to wiggle out of her offer before Cole could refuse. "Since you'll be busy for a while, I thought I might walk down your driveway a bit—I didn't get any real exercise yesterday."

Crutches in place under her arms, Veronica started for the porch door, horribly aware that Cole's eyes followed her every move. She had just reached the door and put out her hand to open it when he spoke.

"If you could help me out, Ronnie, I'd be obliged."

Veronica's hand dropped back down to the crutch grip as she released a small pent-up breath. Trying hard to mask the pleased smile on her lips, she turned.

"What are you planning?" she asked as she made her way over to the sink to wash her hands.

"I've only gotten as far as thawing out four pounds of ground beef. Problem is the boys are getting tired of hamburgers."

Although Veronica cringed at the thought of the "boys" eating nothing but hamburgers, she managed to keep a neutral expression.

"If you have the right ingredients, perhaps a good meat loaf would be better. Do you mind if I look through your cupboards?"

"Go ahead," Cole invited, then began pulling open cupboard doors that held what stores of staples and foods there were. Veronica scanned the shelves, mentally listing the ingredients of one of her favorite recipes.

"I know a recipe for a cheese meat loaf with a sweet topping. If you've got some processed cheese, a couple of carrots and about three large onions, I should be able to make enough meat loaf to last you and your men through two meals." A look of real interest lit Cole's face as he reached for the refrigerator door and brought out the things she'd asked for.

"What kind of vegetables had you planned?"

After a brief discussion of the impromptu menu, Veronica set to work combining the meat loaf ingredients while Cole set the table. Soon there were three large pans of meat loaf in the oven and Veronica began making pastry for pie crusts to contain the lemon pie filling she'd found in the cupboard. For want of a more elaborate, more nutritious dessert for Cole and his men, lemon meringue pie would do.

Cole's men were coming up the path to the porch just as Veronica was cutting generous slices of the steaming meat loaf. Cole carried the vegetables she'd prepared to the table and everything was ready.

"Smells like the boss got us a cook." There was a second of silence before several pairs of heavy boots could be heard thumping up the porch steps and clumping into the kitchen. The room she had once thought so large was suddenly cramped with the entry of Cole's ranch hands.

Five sets of hungry eyes surveyed the modest bounty she'd prepared, then fastened intently on her before the brisk tide of color surging into her cheeks had them glancing away apologetically. She'd forgotten the almost shy reserve many otherwise boisterous cowhands displayed around women. Although none of these men looked familiar to her, their quaint manner of respect and politeness was a quality she found endearing. Belatedly they swept off their hats and glanced expectantly at their boss.

Veronica chanced a look in his direction and saw the cloudy look in Cole's eyes she knew signaled a quick rise of irritation.

"Ain't you gonna make an introduction?" The oldest, shortest, most grizzled-looking cowboy she'd ever seen was the first to speak. "It ain't every day we get a spread like this one served up by a purdy young gal." Wizened brown eyes whipped over to meet Veronica's before they shot back to the boss. "Well?" There was a cantankerousness about the old cowhand that Veronica liked immediately.

"This is Veronica Spencer," Cole began. To Veronica he said, "These are the men who eat at the house every day. Shorty Blake, Ansel Edwards, Bob Brown, Teddy Ferris and Jim Fisher."

Veronica smiled silently at each man, who nodded as he was introduced. Ansel and Shorty, the hand who'd insisted on the introduction, were much older than the other three, with Bob somewhere in his late forties. Teddy and Jim, Veronica guessed, were in their late teens or early twenties.

Once the introductions were made and the men had cleaned up in the washroom just off the hall from the kitchen, they all sat down to eat. Cole seated Veronica to his right, and while the food was passed and plates loaded, the men talked about what they'd accomplished that morning and what Cole's plans for them the rest of the day entailed. Cole also had orders for Shorty to pass along to the three cowhands who had gone to their nearby homes to have lunch with their families.

"Now this is what I call cooking!"

Veronica glanced up, smiling modestly when Shorty's compliment was enthusiastically echoed by the other men around the table. The only one who didn't comment was Cole, who seemed strangely sullen. The only indication the food was to his liking was that he helped himself to generous seconds of everything.

In a surprisingly short time, the table was virtually cleared of food. Cole reached for the pieces of pie on the counter and passed them around, prompting another chorus of approval.

"I'm sure glad you've retired from the kitchen, Boss," Shorty piped up, leaning back in his chair as he patted his slightly protruding paunch with satisfaction. "I run out of Pepto Dismol just this morning." Raucous male laughter burst out, but Cole seemed unamused. "Now that you've hired yourself a good cook, I reckon I can save some money on stomach remedies."

Veronica glanced nervously at Cole. Shorty apparently thought she was their new cook and she felt her face pale. Cole's stony demeanor warned he wasn't pleased with the assumption.

"Veronica is just visiting for a day or two, Shorty. She may only be helping out for this one meal."

Shorty's happy expression fell and he dropped the chair back down onto all four legs. "Well, shucks. D'you mean all we got to look forward to after a spread like this is more of our own cookin'?" The sour expressions on the other men's faces duplicated Shorty's dismay.

"I'm afraid so. Unless that employment agency comes up with someone real soon." Cole stood and picked up his tableware, depositing it into the dishwasher, his brisk manner effectively ending the conversation. One by one his men got up, clearing their own places and adding their dishes to the rapidly filling rack.

"That was a mighty fine meal, Miss Spencer," Shorty told her as he reached for his hat. "It's a cryin' shame you ain't plannin' to stay longer." Veronica couldn't help smiling at the earnest expression on the aging cowhand's weathered face. "A man what cooks like he does—" Shorty jerked a thumb in Cole's direction "—don't deserve to keep good men working for him long."

The solemn rancher he'd just indicated stood with his arms crossed over his broad chest, his mouth twitching with a barely concealed smile.

"I'm not worried about tomorrow, Shorty. It'll be your day to do the cooking." Cole was grinning broadly now at the sour look on Shorty's face.

"Yeah," Shorty groused. "I shoulda guessed my time'd come again before that agency could shake loose with a cook." A disgruntled Shorty ambled to the back door, shaking his head and muttering.

Ansel and Bob grabbed their hats and politely took their leave, but Teddy and Jim were slower about it. Teddy looked as if he was about to say something to her, but Cole loudly cleared his throat and the two each mumbled another bashful compliment about Veronica's cooking and disappeared out the door.

Once they were gone the kitchen took on an uneasy stillness. Veronica was the only person sitting at the table and she rose with as much grace as she could manage, very aware that Cole hadn't taken his eyes off her.

"I think we should have that discussion you wanted so I can be on my way this afternoon." Veronica slipped the crutches beneath her arms and grasped the grips, unconsciously steadying herself for the unpleasantness she expected. Cole said nothing and began to clear the rest of the table. "Should I wait in the den or would you rather talk here?" she prompted.

"We can start here," Cole replied as he worked. "What are your plans for the next few days?" Cole's question was not easily answered, as she hadn't really come to a decision about where she'd be going when she left the ranch. When he looked at her, she shrugged.

"I don't think I'll be going directly back to New York. Charles needs some undivided attention from Mother that he won't get if I'm around." Veronica felt her face redden when Cole's dark brows arched. "No, Charles doesn't like me much, either. Hank was the only one of Mother's husbands who did." She spoke frankly, since this wasn't news to Cole.

"It might be a good idea for me to look for a job until I have the strength and desire to go into business for myself."

"What business is that?"

Veronica tried to gauge whether Cole was really interested or whether he was just making small talk.

"I started an interior-design business with a friend in New York, but after my accident I let her buy me out so she could take on another partner. I'd like to try again in a few months someplace else."

"Not in New York?"

"New York doesn't have much appeal for me beyond the fact that Mother lives there."

"I heard you'd gotten married."

Veronica felt a tremor go through her at the abrupt turn of conversation.

"I did." The words came out surprisingly strong considering she was practically holding her breath, hoping he wouldn't pry further.

"And are you still married?"

At the dreaded question Veronica felt a sudden constriction in her throat and a fresh spasm of pain somewhere in the region of her pride. How she hated to confess even a small part of her failed marriage to Cole and risk the obvious comparison he'd make between her and her mother. Cole waited long moments for her answer, the expression on his face saying he was more than casually interested in her reply.

"No. I'm not married now."

"But you were," he stated persistently, his lips twisting.

"Yes." The admission brought a swift glimmer of hurt into her eyes before they were shielded with a defiant glare. "Go ahead. Say it, Cole," she invited bitterly. "Like mother, like daughter."

"She wasn't much of an example for you, Ronnie."

Veronica's hands clenched on the crutch grips with frustration. What could she say? It was true. Her mother hadn't been a very good influence. But she was not like her mother. Her marriage hadn't ended because of anything she could have humanly controlled. Besides, since their marriage hadn't been consummated it had never been legal anyway. The fact that her big society wedding was followed by an almost instant annulment was too humiliating an experience for her to reveal to Cole. She'd hardly been able to picture herself telling Hank about it, much less Cole with his scorn. It didn't occur to her at that moment that the brokenheartedness she'd felt the past months was now drifting closer to wounded pride.

"If we're going to come to some sort of agreement about your ranch," Veronica said at last, determined to get off the topic of her marriage, "I'd like to get it resolved quickly. The sooner I get to the airport, the sooner I can be on an outgoing flight." She didn't add that she was unaccustomed to standing on her feet in one place for so long and was battling a fatigue she hadn't expected.

At Cole's nod of agreement, she preceded him to the den, her awkward rhythm becoming less and less steady. He seemed not to notice as he gestured at the long leather couch.

Veronica sat down, grateful for the firm comfortable cushioning. Cole tossed a pillow against the end of the couch, but Veronica tried to ignore the thought of how good it would feel to lay her head on that pillow and stretch out for a few minutes. Instead she smothered a yawn behind her hand while Cole's back was still turned toward her. As Cole seated himself in a nearby wing chair the phone shrilled.

Hoping the call would not be lengthy, Veronica dropped her head back, intending to close her eyes for a few seconds. Concentrating on the warm rough sound of Cole's deep voice, she tried to follow the conversation, certain that Cole would soon finish and they could begin the talk he was so determined to have before she left.

Ronnie never knew the exact moment the low full tones of Cole's voice lulled her to sleep. She experienced a sensation of sinking, but it was pleasant, as was the layer of something that someone tucked around her. And when gentle fingers brushed her cheek, the involuntary movement of her head to prolong the contact propelled her far beyond her grasp of reality into the land of perfect dreams.

VERONICA RESISTED AWAKENING, snuggling against the pillow in an effort to cling to the last sleep-induced images: Cole so handsome when he smiled at her that way; the two of them talking long and earnestly, coming closer together; her feeling an overwhelming sense of security; then Cole taking her in his arms and holding her, no longer her adversary but instead . . .

Veronica was suddenly aware of a presence nearby. She opened her eyes to a pair of solemn gray ones that stared down at her face. Startled, disoriented, she struggled up onto one elbow, raking her fingers through her hair.

The eyes belonged to a small dark-haired boy. Their intent study of her face, coupled with a frown and a very familiar quirk of his lips, told her plainly who he was and exactly what he thought of naps.

"You must be Curtis," she said. The child was the image of his father, and Veronica marveled at the likeness. Other than the gray eyes there was almost no resemblance to Jackie she could discern. Veronica offered Curtis a tentative smile, fully expecting the boy to react with one of his own. He did, but it was a very reserved smile, as if he hadn't quite made up his mind about her.

"My name is Veronica," she said as she sat up and began folding the afghan of granny squares that had been placed over her.

"Dad told me to come and see if you were awake." The bare smile had vanished.

"Where is your father?" she asked as she reached for her crutches and prepared to stand. A glance at her watch told her it was after five P.M. How could she have slept so long?

"He's in the kitchen." The boy stepped back and with some curiosity watched her rise before he turned and hurried away. By the time she got to the door, he'd disappeared.

She entered the kitchen moments later, interrupting the conversation Cole was having with a visitor.

"I'm sorry, Cole. I didn't mean to intrude." Veronica had started to turn away when Cole spoke.

"You remember Jackie's sister, Helen, don't you, Ronnie?"

Veronica smiled slightly and nodded, having recognized Helen instantly. She even remembered that Cole had dated the pretty, black-haired Helen for a few weeks before suddenly discovering her younger sister.

"I'd better get going, Cole," Helen said quickly. "Nice to see you again, Veronica," she added in an obvious afterthought as she hurried out the door, leaving Cole staring after her for a long moment.

"I didn't intend to sleep the afternoon away," Veronica ventured. Cole glanced at her, his eyes making a slow sweep of her too-slim frame. "If you wouldn't mind taking my luggage to the car I can be on my way."

"We still need to talk."

"There's really nothing to talk about, Cole. I'll have a lawyer draw up whatever papers are necessary to return my share of the ranch to you."

"Just like that?" The firm lips slanted cynically.

"You could pay for my legal fees," she suggested. Cole's expression turned thunderous and Veronica resisted the urge to mollify him. "I think that's only fair, Cole." She hadn't asked to be given any part of Hank's ranch, and returning it to Cole would save him a fortune. He could easily afford a modest legal fee.

Cole strode across the kitchen to her, a look of incredulous anger on his face. "I'm not going to let you just give it back to me, Ronnie. There's too much money involved!"

Veronica bristled indignantly. "I think I can guess how much money is involved here, Cole. I'm not slow-witted."

Cole raised hard rolled fists and placed them cockily on his trim hips. "All right, Ronnie. Just how much do you guess your share is worth?"

Veronica flushed, feeling like a fool. Unbidden, the memory of the perfect dream she'd had came back on a surge of sweetness that clashed bitterly with reality. She and Cole could never have an earnest talk, they would always be adversaries. The hot color in her cheeks deepened. And Cole would never take her into his arms....

Beneath Cole's glare she suddenly felt like a sixteen-year-old again, never able to win an argument with her stepbrother. Then with astonishing clarity, the old repressed memory of the incident that had guaranteed Cole's everlasting dislike surfaced.

"I figured my share was at least worth Chapman Red," she said.

Her quiet answer wiped the irritation from Cole's strong features. Awash now in recollection, Veronica turned, moved cautiously from the kitchen and on down the hall to her room.

Chapman Red had been Colt's horse, a beautiful bay stallion with a spirit and intelligence that set him apart from the horses Hank had assigned Veronica to ride and care for. Cole had refused to let her ride Red because he believed the big quarter horse was too spirited for a young girl. Veronica had thought Cole selfish and mean, denying her out of spite the pleasure of riding the animal whose affection she coveted.

Weeks of bringing the stallion carrots and other treats and hours on end of sitting on the fence, confiding to Red all her adolescent secrets and heartaches, had forged a special relationship between girl and horse. She could still remember the way Cole used to frown when the big horse whickered a greeting at her, or when Red would trot over to her for a pat when she went near his paddock.

The day finally came when she braved Cole's wrath and took Red for a quick bareback ride just before sundown. She remembered how the pleasure and exhilaration of the ride had evaporated the instant she'd returned to the barn. Cole had come out to check on a mare with an infected cut from barbed wire, and when Veronica rode in, Cole confronted her.

Retribution had been swift, humiliating and painful. Cole had turned her across his knee and spanked her—hard. She had hated him then, hated him fiercely. But the paradox of that hatred was that she'd also desperately needed Cole's affection and admiration.

Yet her desire to ride Chapman Red was so strong that she eventually worked up the courage to defy Cole again. She took Red out for several more rides, and for a time remained undetected. The last ride had been the best. The girl and the stallion, who was so spirited, yet as gentle as a puppy with her, had covered miles, and she had carefully cooled him down on the way home. She had just finished a brisk rubdown, given Red his measure of grain and turned him into his paddock when she heard Cole and Jessie approaching.

Two years older than Veronica, Jessica Ryan lived on the next ranch, and along with half the female population in and around Cheyenne, Jessie had a crush on Cole.

He knew about it, but had been unfailingly indulgent with Jessie while utterly intolerant of Veronica's infatuation.

One look at Ronnie's guilty flush had told Cole she'd been riding his horse again. After the verbal dressing down he gave her in front of Jessie, Ronnie fled to the house.

Later, the unthinkable happened.

Chapman Red had somehow escaped his paddock and raced off to challenge another stallion. One or both of the animals broke the chain on the steel gate of the second enclosure, and the stallion fight that followed left Chapman Red so severely injured he had to be destroyed.

As vehemently as she'd insisted she'd latched Red's gate properly, Cole never believed her and held her completely to blame. Over the years the deep guilt she'd felt at defying Cole by riding his horse had eaten away at her confidence until she, too, had come to believe she had somehow been responsible for the tragedy. Heartsick now at the memory, Veronica leaned against the bedroom door.

"Ronnie?"

She stiffened, then reached for the doorknob to admit Cole, her face a tranquil denial of her inner agony. "While you carry my things out, I'll make certain I haven't left anything behind." As she turned and headed for the bathroom Cole spoke.

"I've got a favor to ask."

His words stopped her and her attention snapped back to his face. Cole's expression was stern but not harsh. She'd expected him to be angry, or at least coldly aloof, but his calm visage was puzzling.

"A favor?"

Cole looked uncomfortable for a moment and she didn't miss the way his gaze dropped to her crutches then to her legs before they returned to her face.

"You don't seem to have any immediate plans," he began. "Of course, I realize you might not be physically able to take much on." Cole paused again. "But the boys were impressed with your cooking and . . ."

Veronica's eyes widened in amazement and a quick smile came and went on her lips. "You want me to cook for you and your men," she concluded, searching Cole's face for any hint that he was joking or she was mistaken.

"You mentioned that cooking was something you're good at and you demonstrated that pretty well at noon. I need someone to fill in until I can get a permanent cook." Cole halted and she sensed he was waiting for some kind of tentative reply from her.

Veronica shook her head. "Oh, Cole, you don't want me here," she scoffed. But even as she tried to get him to admit that, she wished with all her heart he really did want her to stay, if only temporarily. In many ways she was still that adolescent girl who'd craved Cole's acceptance and approval. To her knowledge there had never been anything about her Cole had much use for. But if something as simple as cooking for him while he was in a bind would lessen his hostility, she knew it was an offer she'd find hard to turn down.

"You'd only have to cook, Ronnie. No housework. We've always liked a lot of baked goods and desserts, but we'll settle for good simple meals if you aren't up to any more than that."

Veronica was silent for a few moments considering, trying to honestly gauge her physical ability. Cooking for Cole and his men would be a tiring and time-consuming job. But then, it was only temporary. . . .

"Would I have a free hand with menu planning?"

"Yes, but—" Cole was looking at her almost warily "—we need meals that will stay with us."

Veronica nodded. "I remember how hungry you can get cowboying."

"Then you'll stay on for a while?"

"How long?"

"Until I can find a good cook. And I'll pay you the same wages I'd expect to pay anyone else."

Veronica caught the almost eager sound in his voice but didn't mistake its cause being anything other than it appeared.

"When you find this new cook, will you give me a week's notice, or will you expect me to leave on the next flight to anywhere?" Veronica hadn't been able to suppress the question. She had to keep in mind that Cole had never wanted her around. She knew if he wasn't so desperate for a cook, her luggage would already be in her car and she'd be halfway to Cheyenne.

"I'll give you a week's notice." It seemed to Veronica that he made the concession grudgingly.

"Don't worry, Cole," she began caustically. "I probably won't stay the whole week. I can imagine how charming you'll be when you have no further use for me." Veronica turned away, thinking herself forty kinds of fool, but for the moment more willing to stay than leave. "One thing, though." Her back was to him now.

"What's that?" The ill temper in his voice was easily discernable.

"I don't want you to be rude to my mother if she should call me here. I know you've never liked her, but she—she's been awfully good to me these past few months. If you can't promise me you'll be a model of decorum with her I'll have to turn you down." There was a silence, as if the decision was difficult for him to make. Veronica flicked a look over her shoulder, her violet eyes sparkling with challenge. "Well?"

Cole sighed and shook his head. "I'll be so sweet to your mother she won't crave bonbons for at least a month." Cole wasn't smiling, but the glint of laughter in his eyes filled her with pleasure. The realization that she'd so easily fallen for Cole's subtle charm made her glance nervously at her watch.

"Are leftovers from today's lunch all right with you and your men?" Veronica knew the evening meal was always served promptly at six and it was nearly five-thirty.

"I'll shoot the first one who complains."

CHAPTER THREE

VERONICA DROPPED TIREDLY onto the chair, wincing at her too-abrupt descent. Her whole body ached, and yet she hadn't felt so good about anything in months. Working for Cole the past two weeks had been hard on her, much more physically and emotionally taxing than she had imagined it would be. But she had survived and felt her stamina slowly increasing.

Despite the fact that she had conceded to his wish that she stay, Cole frequently displayed ill humor, questioning everything she did, from the rearranging of the contents of the cupboards and freezers to the lengthy grocery list she'd handed him the first day. But the fact that Cole had ultimately granted her every request indicated he had a fair amount of confidence in her judgment. She learned not to take his gruff manner too seriously.

Veronica's life on the ranch had settled into a routine. She was seeing a therapist in Cheyenne three times a week; no matter how short her stay might be, she couldn't forfeit those sessions. She also found she had more and more time on her hands. In an effort to make the most of it, she had called her mother and arranged for her favorite cookbook and some of her unfinished needlework to be sent, along with the baby quilt she'd started working on for a friend.

In the meantime the employment agency had come up with a woman who wanted to apply for cook. Cole had interviewed her over the phone, then invited her out to prepare the noon meal. At the memory of the most incredibly sloppy-looking woman she'd ever seen, Veronica sighed and shook her head. Just watching her at work in the kitchen had been enough to turn Veronica's stomach. By the time the meal was served, Veronica needed to get out and conveniently "remembered" an errand she had to run in town. She'd returned an hour or so later to find the woman gone and Cole his usual choleric self.

Prospects for the job hadn't improved since then. There had been no other applicants, and according to the woman at the agency, there were likely to be none in the near future.

Cole still refused Veronica's offer to give the ranch and mining stocks to him, and she in turn refused his every monetary counteroffer. They had clearly reached an impasse, so Cole finally let the subject drop. An undeclared truce seemed to have evolved between them and Veronica was delighted. The frequent hostilities and misunderstandings that had marred her time at the ranch years ago, were pleasantly absent now. She and Cole were far from friends, but the fact they were on speaking terms was enough for her.

The low sound of a car coming up the long drive from the highway brought Veronica to her feet. When she heard it pull up in the part of the driveway that curved around the house toward the barn she moved across the kitchen toward the window where she caught sight of a tall leggy blonde getting out of a low, fast-looking sportscar.

"Oh, no." She'd barely given Jessica Ryan a thought since she'd come to the ranch, and because Cole hadn't mentioned the woman, Veronica had just assumed she'd be spared any contact with her. Veronica watched as her childhood nemesis crossed the yard with a fluid grace that mocked her own unavoidable awkwardness.

Tall and model slim, except for her generous bust, Jessie was likely any man's fantasy in the white halter top and shorts that showed off her golden tan to perfection. Now that Cole had been a widower for some time, Veronica wondered if Jessie's old crush on him had brought them into a romantic relationship.

Jessie's perfect mouth bore a sly smirk when she walked into the kitchen as if it were her own. Although she hadn't seen Veronica for years, she made no word of greeting, no polite preamble to the direct confrontation she was apparently determined to have.

"God, Veronica." The amber eyes looked her up and down as if X-ray vision had revealed every scar, every imperfection. Jessie stared at the crutches before at last returning her gaze to Veronica's impassive expression. "No wonder Cole feels sorry for you."

Veronica braced herself against the woman's penchant for cruelty. Jessie Ryan hadn't changed a bit.

"Does he?" she challenged softly, realizing that if Cole felt sorry for her, he certainly hadn't shown it.

"Of course he does. You wouldn't be here otherwise." With a dismissive wave of a manicured hand, Jessie walked to the refrigerator and helped herself to a soft drink. When she'd popped open the can with almost comical care to avoid damaging her long nails, she turned back to Veronica and took a quick sip of her drink.

"Surely you've noticed that Curtis spends very few of his waking hours at this house. He takes all his meals at Helen's, doesn't he?" The well-plucked brows arched. "And Cole hasn't left you alone with Curtis for a second," she surmised, "has he?"

Veronica frowned, unable to deny Jessica's words. Of course she'd noticed, but she'd assumed all that would change when Cole got to know her better, came to trust her fully. Yet Jessie was hammering it all home to her in a way that confirmed the situation would persist for the duration of her stay.

"I hope you haven't started thinking your little Suzy Homemaker act will convince Cole what a wonderful wife you'd make." Jessie laughed as she spoke, but her amber eyes sent quite a different message.

"Why should I?" Veronica hadn't been prepared for this verbal assault, but just as it had been when they were teenagers Jessie always managed to get the upper hand and have the last word.

"Take my advice and forget it. Cole will never trust you alone with Curtis. I'll just bet he'll see to it you two don't even become friendly." Jessie paused for effect. "And Cole would never consider becoming romantically involved with a woman who can't be trusted with his precious son."

Veronica felt her heart constrict as the truth hit home. But before Jessie could claim a sure victory, she rallied. "Jackie's been dead for four years, Jessie, so I guess you'd know better than anyone why Cole hasn't remarried."

There was dead silence. Jessie's flawless features contorted and her cheeks flushed with anger. Veronica remembered well all the many times Jessie had twisted her words, taking malicious delight in the misunderstandings that had been created, especially between Veronica and Cole. It was wickedly satisfying to be able to turn one of Jessie's cruel barbs against her for a change—but Veronica's satisfaction was short-lived.

"You'd better hope Cole finds a permanent cook soon, Ronnie," Jessie warned. "History has a nasty habit of repeating itself." Jessie smiled at the stunned look on Veronica's face. Her good humor once again restored at Veronica's expense, Jessie disappeared out the back door with her can of soda.

Veronica moved out of the kitchen, her weariness forgotten. The mere suggestion that history could somehow be repeated and that she might once again be held responsible for a tragedy terrified her. Without consciously directing her steps, she found herself just outside Hank's bedroom. Assuming Cole would not object if she spent a few minutes inside, Veronica went in.

The room was austere, with its simple functional furniture. Austere, but at the same time warm and comforting, the much-washed wedding-ring quilt that Margaret Chapman had made when she was a teenager enhancing the country charm of the antique bed. A thick layer of dust covered the surfaces of the once lustrous furniture, but Veronica resisted the urge to brush it away. Old habits die hard, and the old habit of never daring to touch without an invitation was deeply ingrained. If only she had stuck to that habit with Chapman Red!

Locked into the bitter memory, her mind automatically went over every detail. As always, Veronica was sure the gate had been latched, the security chain in place. But later, there had been no evidence that the stallion had somehow broken out. Red had never been one of those animals who challenged a gate, so Cole had concluded that Veronica had been careless.

"Damn you!" he had bellowed at her, fury and torment on his face. She could still see the big horse writhing on the ground, sucking in every painful breath.

Veronica squeezed her eyes closed, forcing the recollection to subside. Hank had never believed her negligent. He had told Cole so, and his unshakable belief in her innocence had sparked numerous arguments and brooding silences between father and son. How she'd loved Hank for believing in her!

Veronica wandered around the room looking, resisting the urge to touch the small mementos or tiny gilt-framed photographs on the tall chest. The trunk at the foot of his bed, she knew, held a lifetime of treasures and souvenirs. Hank had let her go through it once, and Veronica's thoughts turned to that happier memory.

"Ronnie!"

Veronica started guiltily at the sound of Cole's voice, then moved quickly to the hall. She had just closed Hank's door when Cole emerged from the kitchen.

"Could you help me with this?" he asked, walking briskly toward her. Veronica's gaze dropped to the hand he extended just before he reached her. Its work-toughened palm, which she assumed had calluses too thick to penetrate, was peppered with scores of splinters that ran across the heel toward the more vulnerable flesh of his wrist. The fact that it was his right hand and Cole was right-handed made her assistance necessary.

"Of course." Veronica followed Cole into his room. When she saw the sewing-machine cabinet sitting in front of the double windows on the outer wall, she was reminded that it had also been the room he'd shared with Jackie. The frilly tieback curtains adorning the windows matched the pastel tones of the ruffles and lace bedspread and canopy, all evidence Cole had changed nothing of the decorating so obviously done by his late wife.

On top of the dresser was a framed photograph of Jackie, side by side with one of Curtis, and Veronica knew without looking that Jackie's clothing would still be hanging in the huge closet that held Cole's clothes, that her personal things probably still took up several drawers. It dawned on her that just as Hank's room was a kind of shrine, Cole's bedroom was a shrine to Jackie.

Strange how she'd never imagined him capable of real love—the sort he'd evidently had for Jackie and the sort he must have for his son. Now she realized she was wrong. And until that conversation with Jessie, she'd assumed Cole was keeping his son from having any close contact with her because of sheer possessiveness rather than the protectiveness shown by a loving father.

Jessie's remark about Cole's precious son had been accurate. Just as Jackie had been precious and much loved by this harsh rancher who could summon so little affection for Veronica, young Curtis was likely loved to distraction. Veronica felt guilty that her presence here was costing Cole time with the boy. At Curtis's age, that time was far too valuable to miss.

Veronica watched as Cole whipped off his hat and began rummaging in the medicine cabinet for tweezers and peroxide. A quick scan of the large bathroom told her that only Cole's things were scattered around the somewhat untidy interior. When her eyes came back to his, he was watching her with a shrewdness that made her gaze shy away. It was as if he'd been aware of her observation and wondered what she thought. *That's ridiculous,* she chided herself. *Cole doesn't care what I think.*

"Where would be most comfortable for you to work?" he asked, and she glanced around the room for a well-lit spot. Instead of waiting for her decision, Cole was already clearing a space on the counter top next to the sink. "Sit here."

Veronica eyed the counter with some misgiving, then decided it was the best place for light. She set her crutches aside and had just turned her back to the counter to use her arms to lever herself up when Cole's big hands spanned her small waist.

"Cole—your hand!" She reached to gently push it away so that the wood slivers wouldn't become more deeply imbedded.

"Never mind. I can do this." With far more ease than she could have managed alone, Cole lifted her onto the counter. Then bracing a lean hip against the counter top by her knee, he held his injured hand over her lap.

The instant her fingers came into contact with Cole's warmth, a tremor of sensation sped up her arm. Her worried gaze shot up to meet the dark glimmers in Cole's cobalt-blue eyes. Cole stared back, seemingly oblivious to the warm shock she'd just experienced. Instead, his gaze dropped to her barely parted lips. Flustered, Veronica returned her attention to his hand and carefully inspected the wood slivers, some of them driven in so deeply they had drawn blood.

"How did you do this?" Veronica asked, reaching for the tweezers to begin plucking out the largest of the fragments.

"The colt I was working with this afternoon decided he'd like me a whole lot better if I was on the other side of the fence. Damn near threw me over the top rail." Visibly alarmed, Veronica glanced up, only to meet Cole's grin. "I grabbed the fence post and broke my fall, but I ended up with a hand full of splinters."

Veronica felt a smile tug at her mouth. Cole and his father always made the worst spills sound like high comedy.

"Next time, I'll wear my gloves."

Veronica stared a moment more, realizing how powerful her attraction to Cole really was. Uneasy with the thought, she lowered her head and got back to work.

Taking out one of the larger splinters, she glanced around for someplace to deposit it. Cole reached for the small towel that hung on the rack by her shoulder, and laid it across her lap, indicating she could use that. Veronica worked on in silence, intent on what she was doing. Occasionally she angled Cole's big hand so that the light hit it more directly, but she worked steadily.

Yet for all her outward competence and seeming concentration, her senses were awash with the man. The press of his hip against her knee, the warm hard feel of his hand, the dizzying nearness when his head brushed hers while they both watched her work. Then there was the tantalizing male scent of him, something that aftershave and soap only heightened. With every breath her senses became heightened, and for the first time in her life, she considered initiating a kiss.

The instant the thought came to mind she almost groaned. She would be out of this house in ten minutes, cook or no, if Cole even suspected what was going on in her mind. How he'd hated her infatuation with him all those years ago! Now that she had grown up, he would appreciate it even less.

"What are you thinking?"

Veronica jerked, unintentionally driving one of the larger splinters deeper.

"I'm sorry, Cole—you startled me." It was half the truth anyway. Yet Cole hadn't pulled his hand away or lost his temper. Instead he was being more than patient with her as he continued to let his hand rest lightly in the palm of hers. Veronica forced her attention back to her work.

"Are you going to let my question pass?"

Veronica glanced up, surprised that he was pursuing a conversation with her. She paused and considered for a moment. Perhaps this was a good time to broach the subject of his son. While she went back to pulling out splinters, she tried to assess the best way of bringing the subject up, then resolved to be direct.

"I was just thinking that you've sacrificed a lot of time with your son since I've been here." Cole's hand tensed slightly, but didn't withdraw. "Children grow so fast, Cole, and Curtis is still at an age neither of you can afford to miss."

"So?" It wasn't the belligerent comeback she'd half expected, but it betrayed annoyance nonetheless.

"So, I thought you might think about having Curtis home more while I'm here, if I promise to keep my distance from him." There was no change this time in the tension of Cole's hand and no verbal indication that he'd even heard what she'd said. "I think I can be a friendly presence in his home without courting his friendship," she went on. "Besides, if you're together as much as you both need to be, Curtis won't even notice I'm anything more important than an appliance or a piece of furniture."

"That's enough!" Cole's voice was a gritty hiss. Violet eyes, wide with apprehension, shot up to stormy blue ones. Cole was angry now. Intuition told her he was angry because she'd voiced aloud the very conditions he would have dictated himself if he hadn't thought he'd feel so guilty doing it. She opened her mouth to brazenly suggest just that, but his free hand came up to touch her cheek and a thumb pressed gently over her soft lips. Its hard pad rested partially on her teeth, setting off a primitive reaction deep inside her. Not even Eric's passionate kisses produced such a deeply thrilling response in her. Yet Cole had breeched her reserve with a mere touch. Frightened at what that might mean, Veronica pushed his hand away.

"Do you want me to finish this or not?" she demanded. Now she was the one who was irritable.

"I'd appreciate it," came the reply. "Please, Veronica."

Those last words invaded her confused irritation and warmed her all the way to her heart. She set to work again, searching out the remainder of the splinters, then wiping the tweezers clean on the towel. Her stirred-up feelings settled finally, but her acute awareness of Cole didn't subside.

Cole's awareness of her hadn't abated, either. She had no way of knowing that the gruff rancher was just noticing the subtle red glints in her dark hair and letting his gaze wander at will over her classically shaped features. Persistently the cobalt-blue eyes were attracted to her lips, watching her moisten them occasionally. He had been just as surprised as she at his own reaction to the feel of her soft lips and the smooth surface of her teeth beneath his thumb. He couldn't remember a time in the four years since his wife's death when he wanted to taste a woman the way he wanted to taste Veronica. The urge to do so was increasing with every passing moment.

Veronica finished with the tedious removals, then tenderly rechecked for any she might have missed. Satisfied she'd got every one, she reached for a gauze pad from the box Cole had set out and moistened it with peroxide. Again and again she wiped the treated gauze over the tiny slits, watching them turn white with cleansing bubbles before she smeared on an antibiotic cream. When she finished, she taped a fresh gauze pad over the area to keep out the dirt.

Cole didn't step away, maintaining contact with her knee while she twisted the caps back on the peroxide bottle and cream tube and closed the box of gauze pads. She'd inched her leg away from his hip and started to ease herself off the edge of the counter when Cole's hand shot out to stop her.

"Thank you, Ronnie."

Veronica looked up in time to see his dark head already making a slow descent, closing the few inches between their lips. At the last second, she somehow found the strength to turn her face away. The kiss caught the corner of her mouth and lingered.

"I thought you'd welcome this," he murmured, his lips grazing her cheek. Veronica was unable to formulate a believable denial. A leaden sensation was invading every muscle and her thoughts were evaporating.

"But you don't even—" *like me,* she tried to get out, but the belated attempt was a waste as Cole's mouth settled over her lips, catching them parted. Emotion flooded her heart and shot its fluid heat to the very depths of her femininity. It was as if a flash fire was bursting inside her and she was helpless to stop herself from wrapping her arms around Cole's neck and kissing him back. Nothing in her entire experience had prepared her for this. Eric's kisses had been dull by comparison, and the imagination of her teen years hadn't had the sophistication to conjure up more than a fraction of this reality. If she had been rational, she could have reminded herself that even as an adult, she hadn't acquired the kind of experience necessary to foresee this.

Cole made a husky sound deep in his throat and his lips slipped off hers to glide enticingly toward her ear. Playful nips elicited an unwilling sigh of pleasurable torment.

"Has it been a while, Ronnie?" asked Cole, as his warm breath caressed her ear.

The sigh of delight caught in her throat. Another tender love nip distracted her briefly as he went on, "It's been a long time for me, too."

Inexperienced though she was, Veronica suddenly knew exactly what Cole was asking and she went rigid in his arms. To discourage the resistance he sensed, Cole's lips found hers again.

Neither of them heard the soft footfalls coming through Cole's bedroom or the shocked gasp that came from the doorway. "I think I'd better come back later."

Cole's lips didn't abruptly abandon hers, but Veronica felt his passion die as embarrassment overcame hers. Keeping her in his arms, Cole glanced over his shoulder at his sister-in-law.

"Afternoon, Helen." Cole eased Veronica off the counter before he turned fully to the brunette whose dark eyes shifted from Veronica's pink-tinged cheeks to Cole's expressionless face. "Hello, Jessie."

Veronica's discomfort increased as Jessie stepped into view.

"I was just coming over to ask a favor of Veronica when Jessie came up from the barn saying she'd heard you'd been hurt." The confused concern on Helen's face gave way to disapproval when her dark eyes skittered toward Veronica.

"Yes, darling." Jessie crowded her way past the brunette. "It's not serious, is it?" Her amber eyes were all over Cole before they shot directly to Veronica's slightly puffy lips.

"Ronnie has taken care of it."

"I can see she has." Jessie's dusky voice was just a tone above a growl, but she turned her sweetest smile on Cole as she reached to take him by the arm, effectively separating Veronica from him as she wedged her long perfect body between them. "Now that your injury is tended to, how about showing me that filly you promised?" How quickly the cattiness had changed to something more like baby talk. Veronica was sickened.

"Excuse me." Veronica inched toward the door and Helen stepped aside to give easier passage. Self-consciously Veronica moved through the bedroom to the hall, then made for the kitchen.

Once there, she could no longer hear Jessie's cooing voice. There was a faint murmur of conversation, but Veronica managed to block out even that sound as she briskly unloaded the dishwasher and tried to distract her mind and her body from the aftereffects of Cole's kiss.

Only now was she fully aware of how unexpected that kiss had been. Never in a million years would she have believed it could happen. Not with Cole. Not with any man, she reminded herself. When Eric abandoned her, he'd stripped her of any confidence she might have possessed about her sexual attractiveness. For what man could ever find her scarred body desirable?

"I'll be down at the barn, Ronnie." Cole came through the kitchen, his dusty black Stetson firmly in place. Veronica felt herself impaled by his riveting blue eyes, which told her nothing of his thoughts before they swung away. Jessie dogged his steps, her bow-shaped mouth pursed in annoyance at the pace Cole set. Helen followed the pair in, but when Cole and Jessie went out the back door, she stayed behind.

"You had a favor to ask?" Veronica invited the woman to speak, hoping Helen wouldn't mention anything about seeing her and Cole kissing. Veronica remembered Helen, who was nearly Cole's thirty-four years, as being cool but polite. Neither Helen nor Jackie had ever had much time for her. It wasn't that they'd slighted her, but both of them had been older and much more housebound than she. For most of her two years on the ranch Veronica had been an unabashed tomboy, and she'd had little in common with the sisters.

"I was wondering if you'd make a couple of the dishes I've planned for the barbecue I'm having tomorrow night." Helen was smiling pleasantly. "Cole mentioned what a good cook you are and suggested you might consider helping me out if you're up to it." Veronica felt herself relax, absurdly pleased that Cole had complimented her to someone. "Jackie and I used to do this every year and, well, after she passed away, Hank's cook always helped out. You don't need to feel obligated, Veronica, but I could sure use your help."

"I'll be glad to help, Helen. Just tell me what you want and I'll make it."

"Good. Thank you. I'll send home the food and recipes with Cole when he comes for Curtis." Helen paused, and the pleasant smile turned cool. "And there's something else I'd like to ask."

Veronica waited, not smiling either. She could guess what was coming, and she fervently wished Helen would just let the incident pass without comment. "What's that?"

"I think perhaps you should talk to Cole about moving you into that small vacant house between here and the highway, the one that's usually assigned to the ranch's cook. I don't think it's good for Curtis to live in a house where there are two single adults sleeping within a few feet of each other." Helen at least had the grace to blush.

"And after what I just saw, I think it's even more imperative."

Veronica stared, knowing Helen was overreacting but that her firm tone signaled she would tolerate no dissent. Until now Veronica hadn't really given much thought to the propriety of living under the same roof as Cole. She wasn't too concerned about her reputation or Cole's, either, since nothing was going on between them.

Interpreting Veronica's initial silence as resistance, Helen went on, "I know Cole is a very attractive man, Ronnie, so maybe he's a lot of temptation for you—you had such a crush on him once." Helen smiled tolerantly at the tides of color that washed into Veronica's cheeks. "Sometimes those lovesick feelings resurrect themselves at awkward times when we grow older. But once you get settled someplace where you're not in such close contact with Cole, I'm certain you'll regain some perspective."

Veronica nearly choked with outrage. She stood quietly for a few moments before she trusted herself to speak, her hands clenched so tightly on the crutch grips they tingled.

Veronica tried valiantly to match Helen's cool. "Cole would be the first to remind you that what goes on in his home is his business," she said. "But if you feel so strongly about my presence here, then by all means speak to Cole about it. I'll abide by any decision he makes."

Helen looked a bit dismayed before she recovered. "But you should be the one to speak to Cole."

"There's nothing between Cole and me, Helen, and I'm not about to suggest to him that I think there is by asking him to move me out of this house." Veronica was trembling, hating the angry humiliation she felt. "Now if that's all, I've got a lot to do before the evening meal."

Helen left without another word. Veronica turned back to the cupboard, distressed that she'd just made another enemy.

And for what? One silly, impossibly thrilling kiss? Veronica sighed. Despite what Helen and probably Jessie had seen and despite what she'd felt in those brief moments of ecstasy, there had been no indication from Cole that his kiss had been anything more for him than a mere sensual impulse.

CHAPTER FOUR

AFTER SUPPER, when Cole came home with Curtis and the food and recipes from Helen, Veronica managed to be conveniently absent from the house. She was in the side yard out of sight of the driveway, carefully poking about the ill-tended flowerbeds to see if any perennial blooms had managed to survive the weeds. When Cole and Curtis went inside, she moved around to the front of the house, then decided to make her way down a portion of the long driveway that wandered in a lazy arc to the highway more than a mile away.

The warm evening air was laden with dust from the recent passing of Cole's car, but Veronica cared little that it settled over her clothing or found beads of perspiration to cling to. She was thinking about the awful tension at supper more than an hour earlier. Cole had been terse with his men to the point of rudeness, and he'd barely acknowledged Veronica's presence. There could have been no clearer indication of how much he regretted his impulse that afternoon, or how anxious he was to disabuse her of any notion that it had meant anything to him. His aloofness reminded her of his initial attempts to ignore her infatuation with him years ago.

Veronica cringed at the memory of the time she'd so foolishly confessed her love to Cole. He had not taken to a brotherly role, the fifteen-year-old Veronica had reasoned, so perhaps he didn't think of her that way. And when Cole looked at her—as he had occasionally—with neither irritation nor dislike, she'd begun to think he'd secretly found himself liking her as a woman. That was all the encouragement Cole's adoring little stepsister had needed to try out her newly discovered feminine wiles.

Incautious and inexperienced, the young Veronica began to flirt with Cole when they were alone. Cole ignored her amateur attempts to imitate what she'd seen her mother do so often, until he finally got tired of having Veronica constantly under foot.

"But I love you, Cole," she declared, with all the melodramatic intensity only a lovesick adolescent can portray. But he just laughed at her and told her she had a particularly bad case of puppy love. The scorn in his laughter hurt deeply. He didn't even like her enough to rebuff her in a way that left her with any self-respect. In daring retaliation, knowing that Cole had no use for her as a sister or a lover, she had ridden Chapman Red for the first time.

Preoccupied with her memories, Veronica made a misstep but deftly regained her balance. She'd already managed the prescribed half-mile daily walk, and the physical therapist had cautioned her not to push herself and risk the possibility of a setback. Since the last operation, she'd had fewer and fewer muscle spasms and she certainly didn't want to spoil her record. Reluctantly she turned toward the house and started making her way back, curious about what recipes Helen had sent over for her to prepare.

JUST AFTER BREAKFAST the next day, Veronica started to clean and prepare the enormous amount of fresh vegetables Helen intended to serve with the four sour-cream based dips Veronica had mixed the night before. The three-dozen eggs that had been boiled lay chilling in the refrigerator, waiting to be deviled. Veronica was disappointed that there was little to be done that challenged her cooking skills.

"Helen didn't give you much more than busy work to do, did she?" Cole whipped off his hat and tossed it carelessly toward the coat tree in the corner as he came in the porch door. Veronica noticed that he'd discarded the bandage on his hand.

"There's a lot of busy work involved when you cook for a crowd," Veronica replied noncommittally. "I don't mind." Cole crossed the room to the coffee pot.

"Is this my coffee or yours?" he asked, referring to the expensive decaffeinated brand Veronica preferred.

"Yours," Veronica said, trying not to let Cole's presence in the kitchen throw her off balance. It was the first time since yesterday afternoon that they had been alone together and Veronica was battling an impossible longing for his nearness.

With a small shock, she realized that her feelings for Cole weren't motivated as much by the leftovers of her adolescent crush on him as by the much more complicated, full-blown longings of a woman who wanted the companionship and intimacy of a special man. That realization sent her gaze skittering in his direction. Cole had poured himself some coffee and was sipping it, the hint of a satisfied smile on his mouth as he tasted the rich dark brew.

Those were the same firm sensual lips that had so thoroughly possessed hers less than twenty-four hours ago. The long tanned fingers that dwarfed the coffee cup were the ones that had reached for her and combed through her hair with gentle ferocity. Helplessly her eyes traced the snug fit of his chambray work shirt and worn denim jeans, overwhelmed by the sudden memory of what that lean hard body had felt like beneath her hands.

Veronica had to look away. This intense physical longing was something she'd never experienced, and that Cole had so quickly brought it to the surface signaled the potential for a far more devastating hurt than the one Eric had inflicted on her.

"You haven't heard a word I've said." Cole's deep rough voice intruded on her troubled thoughts in gentle accusation.

"What?"

"I asked if you wanted to ride over to Helen's with Curtis and me this evening." Veronica's knife halted in midair, then came down on a helpless stalk of celery with finality.

"No, thank you." Veronica didn't mention that Helen had neglected to invite her. Until she did, Veronica would take nothing for granted.

"Good coffee, Ronnie." Cole strode from the kitchen, leaving Veronica with an irrational wish that he'd found some reason to stay longer.

"VERONICA!"

Cole's thundering voice from the front yard brought her quickly from the kitchen just as she slid the cake she'd just mixed into the oven. A delivery truck was parked out front. Veronica thought she'd heard an engine earlier, but she'd been running the mixer off and on and hadn't paid much attention.

"Oh good." Veronica smiled at the large box that had been left on the porch. The delivery man had just climbed back into his truck and was driving away. "I didn't expect this until sometime next week," she explained hastily to her iron-faced stepbrother as she went through the screen door onto the porch.

"Would you mind carrying this box to the kitchen for me?" she asked as she stepped aside and held the porch door open expectantly. Cole didn't move and his stern expression didn't alter a whit. Veronica's smile thinned to a slight line.

"What's in it?" Cole eyed her curiously, but Veronica missed the gentle look that had come over his face at the defensive stiffening of her thin shoulders.

"Just a cookbook and some needlework," she told him, forcing herself to look at him. "And before you jump to any conclusions, that doesn't mean I'm planning to move in permanently."

Veronica turned awkwardly and went back inside. Cole followed a few steps behind her, his booted feet the only other sound in the house as she moved stiffly into the kitchen.

"Where do you want this?" came the gruff question and Veronica relaxed, recognizing the hint of gentleness that softened his deep voice.

"On the table," she answered, then cautioned, "but be careful, I've got a cake in the oven." In no time, Cole had the taped seam sliced open, and Veronica began unpacking the box, looking for the cookbook.

"What's that?" Cole's attention was fixed on the large plastic bag of hexagon quilt patches that Veronica had lifted out of the box.

"A baby quilt." Cole's eyes jumped up to meet hers, his gaze intense. "It's for a friend of mine whose baby is due in another month," she explained. "I thought I'd work on it while I'm here."

"Does that go with it?" Cole gestured toward the huge wooden quilting hoop she was taking out and Veronica nodded. He watched as she pulled out quilt bat and fabrics, a couple of partially completed needlework projects and sewing supplies before she came to the large, loose-leaf cookbook she was after.

"Do you know what to do with all that?"

Veronica was irritated by the faint incredulity in Cole's voice. "That's right. Astonishing, isn't it?" Veronica turned toward the cupboard and placed her cookbook next to the meager collection at the back of the counter.

"Discounting the fact that your mother couldn't teach you things like this, I'd say you have a few old-fashioned hobbies for a woman of the eighties. Aren't you one of those liberated females who wants a career and a sophisticated life-style—husband and children be damned?"

"Careful, Cole. Your chauvinism is showing." But the look she flashed over her shoulder was indulgent. Cole was an old-fashioned male, but from what Hank had told her, she'd got the impression that Cole had always encouraged Jackie to use her talents and be all she was capable of being.

Veronica turned back toward the box, noticing uneasily that Cole was waiting for her to answer his question. Flustered, she began putting all the sewing supplies back in the box while she considered her reply. A quick glance upward caught Cole's speculative gaze.

"After so many years of not having a family or any real home, having a husband and children and making a good home is more important to me than having an outside career." Veronica shrugged as if the disclosure was not the deep confession it really was. Suddenly overcome with heartache, she looked down at the box. She had thought she'd have all that with Eric Marshall. "And you can find classes that teach you to do just about anything these days," she added airily. Veronica forced a smile onto her lips and met Cole's ever-watching eyes. "What would you like for supper?"

"You've got tonight off." Cole's stern visage relaxed.

"That's right. I guess I forgot." Veronica paused, then decided to ask Cole about something while they were getting along. "I was wondering if you'd mind letting me use Jackie's sewing machine." His gaze darted from hers and Veronica instantly regretted asking.

"That's all right," she assured him hastily. "I can piece the quilt by hand. In fact, it might be easier to work with if I did. Besides, that overstuffed chair by the lamp in the living room is far more comfortable than a straight chair."

Cole's eyes turned a stormy blue. "Stop walking on eggshells around me, Ronnie."

Veronica's mouth fell open at the gruff order.

"And don't look so surprised. Hell, you'd think I was some kind of tyrant the way you act," he grumbled.

"Don't swear."

"It's my house and my temper. I'll swear if I want to," he thundered, but the suggestion of a smile had reached his lips, a companion to the sparkle of laughter in his eyes. The world had brightened considerably. "The instruction book for the sewing machine is in one of the drawers," he said, his voice lowering. "You're welcome to it any time as long as I'm not sleeping. And watch where you drop your pins. I'm still finding Jackie's."

Veronica smiled at Cole's false ferocity, marveling at the friendliness between them and loving it. "Thank you, Cole."

"You might not be thanking me if you suddenly find yourself stuck with the mending," he warned.

"Oh, no, I won't," Veronica teased. "You promised me I was only hired to cook, nothing else."

Cole growled good-naturedly, then said, "I was a desperate man then. I hadn't had a decent home-cooked meal for weeks and I was probably delirious." He grinned at Veronica's skeptical smirk. "If you'll let me renegotiate our agreement to include mending, I promise to come up with a bribe you'll like better than a raise—not that you can't have a raise instead," he added quickly. "The boys already think I got the better part of our first deal," he told her. "Will you think about it?" Veronica giggled at Cole's earnest expression.

"As long as you don't deluge me with mending, I'll do it in return for the use of the sewing machine. Forget about any deals or bribes."

"You're really quite a pleasant surprise, Veronica." Cole's low rough voice warmed her and she felt her emotions scramble to harden themselves against the appeal of Cole's long-awaited approval. The small-scale inner war she'd been waging against allowing the compellingly deep feelings she had for Cole to blossom naturally into love suffered a severe setback at the affection behind his words.

She made some inane comment about flattery then that casually brushed off Cole's remark. She couldn't even remember what it was the moment after she'd said it, but was just grateful when she could finally retreat to the quiet sanctuary of her room.

THE PHONE RANG STRIDENTLY in the quiet house and Veronica rose from the sewing machine without her crutches and with stiff caution covered the few feet to the telephone extension on Cole's night table.

"Chapman Ranch."

"Are you all right, Ronnie?" Cole's voice betrayed a concern that threw her for a moment.

"Of course I'm all right," she assured him. "What could be wrong?"

"I was afraid you'd had car trouble or something. What's taking you so long to get here?"

Confused and surprised by Cole's impatient tone, she was slow to answer.

"I'm not coming to Helen's," she said quietly.

"What did you say?" The sound of the party came clearly over the connection.

"I'm not coming," she repeated.

"What do you mean, you're not coming?"

"I wasn't invited," she told him truthfully, her fingers twisting the phone cord.

"Maybe Helen didn't send you an engraved invitation but you were invited," Cole stated confidently.

"When?" Veronica released the phone cord to massage her forehead wearily.

"When she spoke to you about helping her out, I suppose."

Veronica's mouth twisted in grim amusement.

"Has she asked you where I am tonight?" she challenged. There was a second's silence.

"Well, no. But she's been busy," he hastened to add. "I'll be there in ten minutes to pick you up. Be ready."

"Don't, Cole," she warned. "It will be a wasted trip. I'm not about to go to Helen's." Veronica took a deep breath. "I wouldn't come to Helen's even if I had been invited."

"Why not?" Cole was angry now.

Veronica frantically tried to think of some reason that would not put him at odds with his sister-in-law. She hadn't mentioned the confrontation she'd had with Helen the day before. Veronica squeezed her eyes closed.

"You know me," she began, letting just the right touch of snobbery affect her soft voice. "I'm afraid Helen's little get-together is just a little too down-home for my uptown taste." Veronica winced at the lie. "But you and Curtis have a good time," she enthused before she dropped the phone into its cradle, not wanting to hear Cole's temper explode.

Veronica made her way back to the sewing machine and methodically picked up the quilt pieces and sewing supplies. She folded the machine into its cabinet and prepared to take her things back to her room. A good long bath and an early night would shorten the lonely evening considerably.

CHAPTER FIVE

VERONICA TOOK HER WALK early the next morning, and feeling fit and increasingly stronger, she decided to double the prescribed distance. Cole and Curtis would probably spend the day at Helen's, she thought, and Cole's men didn't come to the house for meals on Sundays. It was supposed to be her day off, but she planned to spend the afternoon baking. Although the weather forecasters were predicting a hot day, the central air conditioning in the house would enable her to work comfortably.

Her walk completed, Veronica was just stepping onto the porch when Curtis burst out the back door, brushing past her in a flurry of motion that had her turning to watch his strong young legs carry him swiftly toward the barns. She had just turned back toward the door when the soft smile evaporated from her lips. Cole was staring at her stonily from beneath the black brim of his Stetson.

"Good morning, Cole."

"Good morning, Miss Uptown," he mocked. Veronica couldn't maintain contact with the harshness in Cole's gaze and she glanced away. She had started to step aside for Cole to pass when he reached for her chin and lifted her face to his scrutiny.

"I've got a pretty good idea that you and Helen haven't exactly hit it off," he growled. "But if you ever tell a wild tale like you did last night about being too up-

town, I'm going to turn you across my Neanderthal knee
and warm your backside.'' Veronica was unprepared for
the brief hard kiss that followed his warning. Cole's lips
released hers and he bounded down the stairs to catch up
with his son, leaving Veronica in an emotional whirlwind of pleasure and relief.

Later that day, just as she removed the last of the
chocolate-chip cookies from the oven, Veronica heard the
muffled jangle of spurs and the harsh snort of a spirited
horse out back. When she heard Cole come up the porch
steps, she hurriedly slipped the last of the cookies onto
the cooling rack and switched off the oven. Cole was just
coming through the door as she turned to put the mixing
bowls and utensils into the dishwasher.

"Are you finished in here for a while?" he asked, then
spied the cookies. Veronica caught the look and smiled.

"Help yourself."

"Mmmm." Cole's eyes were lit with appreciation as he
savored the taste of a warm cookie. "Wait till Curtis gets
wind of these."

"There might not be any left," Veronica laughed as
Cole wrapped a couple of cookies in a napkin and put
them into his shirt pocket.

"Come on outside with me. I have a surprise for you."
He crossed to the porch door and held it open for her.
Veronica reached for her crutches and readily complied.
She was well onto the porch when her heart seemed to
come to a stop. Cole strode past her, descended the stairs
and picked up the trailing reins of a horse.

The sight of the big bay stallion struck at her heart with
the force of a physical blow. Instantly eight years
dropped away and she was once again the stepsister, the
intruder who'd coveted everything Cole Chapman loved,
particularly the big stallion with hide the color of blood.

"Are you coming?"

Cole's voice snapped her back to the present and she felt her balance waver.

"What?"

Cole studied her with a frown, tipped his hat back, then repositioned it and tugged the brim lower.

"I promised to bribe you into doing the mending. Of course, another benefit of getting you on a horse again is that riding will help strengthen your legs. Spending more time in the fresh air should bring some color back into those cheeks and help out that puny appetite of yours."

Veronica felt the lump in her throat thicken. She suddenly felt weak and leaned most of her weight on her crutches. A tremor started in her knees and worked its way into every joint until she feared she'd collapse.

"I don't...ride anymore."

"I talked to your mother about it earlier this morning and she said your therapist back in New York had recommended horseback riding." Veronica was too stunned to take in that Cole had consulted her mother about anything.

"I haven't ridden a horse in years and I—I'm not interested anymore," she managed, nearly strangling with unshed tears. "I've got work to do inside." Ronnie's haste made her feel more awkward than usual as she turned to make a quick retreat.

"Ronnie?" The pulsing roar of blood in her ears obscured the concern in Cole's voice.

"I'm going in," she choked out, then tugged sharply on the screen door. She didn't return to her baking. Instead, she moved as quickly as she could to the hall, anxious to get to her room.

Once there, she closed the door and leaned a shoulder against it. The tears had started, but when she heard her name being called from the kitchen she wiped them away impatiently with the back of her hand. She then crossed the room to the bath and through the window caught sight of the bay horse standing riderless with his reins wrapped around a porch pillar. In moments, she had jerked the shades closed.

"Ronnie?" Cole had come into her room.

"Get out!" Veronica began shaking, unable to comprehend the reason Cole was inflicting this punishment on her. She edged toward the bathroom door, wanting only to escape Cole's astonished expression.

Cole was striding boldly closer, reaching for Veronica when she pressed herself against the wall in an effort to avoid his touch. One of her crutches clattered to the floor when she tried to shake off his gentle grip.

"Come for a ride. Just down to the barn. I'll walk beside you." Cole's voice had an eerie stillness to it.

"I don't ride anymore. I told you that." Veronica's other crutch fell to the floor as she gripped Cole's wrist in self-protection. His expression softened.

"How long has it been, Ronnie? How long have you stayed away from horses?" Cole paused when he saw tears streak down her flushed cheeks. "Your mother seemed to think that you haven't gone near a horse since you lived here." Cole's voice was a husky rasp. "Is that true?"

Veronica felt her body wilt and she sagged miserably against the wall. She couldn't look at him.

"The half-wild little tomboy I knew ate, slept and dreamed horses," Cole kidded gently. "She didn't swear off them, did she?"

Veronica's eyes squeezed closed and she nodded, missing the bleak look that came into Cole's eyes.

"Why?" he rasped. Veronica shook her head, her delicate features crumpling. It was a long moment before she could speak.

"I was so sure I'd fastened that gate. I could have sworn..." Veronica's soft voice lapsed into a childlike sob and Cole drew her into his strong arms.

"Have you been punishing yourself all these years?" Cole demanded in a gruff whisper. "Hmm?" His arms tightened promptingly.

"I was untrustworthy... careless," she mumbled disconsolately into Cole's warm shirt front.

He gripped her chin and forced her to look up at him. "You said at the time you could have sworn you'd fastened the gate—that you clearly remembered latching it and fastening the security chain," he reminded her.

"And I believed it, Cole. I believed it with all my heart." The tortured violet eyes fluttered closed in anguish. "But I must have been wrong. Red died and I was the last one with him." Cole pulled her against himself again and she heard him curse softly.

"Listen to me, Ronnie." The sternness in his voice insured her full attention. "You weren't the only person around the barn that day. Anyone could have forgotten to make sure that gate was properly latched." Cole held her away from his chest to see her face, but her eyes shied away. "I never should have accused you like I did," he grumbled. "And I never wanted to deprive you the pleasure of horses." Fresh tears slid down her damp cheeks and Cole's voice softened.

"I'm sorry, Ronnie. You were just a kid and I was too hard on you. You loved that horse even more than I did, didn't you?" Veronica nodded and gave a half sob of agreement. Cole cuddled her against his broad chest and rested his chin on top of her head. "Angry as I was then, I never once thought you'd punish yourself this way."

When Veronica pressed her hands against Cole's chest and tried to push away, he let her. "Why are you being so nice, Cole?" Veronica's spine stiffened. "Do you feel sorry for me?" She didn't want his apology if he did. Veronica studied Cole's face while he seemed to consider her question.

"No. I don't feel sorry for you, Ronnie," he said at last. "But I've come to regret a lot of things that happened between you and me back then. Looking back on those two years, I realize now that I never really gave you a chance." Cole repositioned his hat in a betrayal of his unease. "I guess in that way I do feel sorry for you," he admitted. "Is it too late for us to be friends?"

Veronica could scarcely believe what she was hearing.

"If that's what you want," she answered unsteadily.

"Is it what you want?" he countered, a half smile lifting the corners of his mouth.

"Yes," she admitted shyly and her gaze wavered. She didn't want Cole to see the joy in her eyes that might have revealed how much she'd always wanted the two of them to be friends, more than friends....

"Then come on," he urged. Veronica started to comply by putting her hand into the strong tanned one he held out for her, but then she hesitated, remembering the crutches that lay on the floor at their feet. Cole's gaze followed hers and he leaned down to pick them up before she could.

"Uh-oh." Belatedly Cole tried to catch the small crumbs of cookie that slipped out of his shirt pocket. When he straightened, his lips formed a wry line as he slipped his fingers into the pocket and felt the crumbled

remains. The solemnity of the past few minu...
lifted. Veronica started to grin, then found her
laughing with Cole.

"Wait a minute." Cole handed her the crutches and
moved into the bathroom. She listened to the sound of
running water before he came back with a warm wet
washcloth, which he used to tenderly brush the dark half
circles of mascara from beneath her eyes and smooth
away the gray tear trails from her cheeks. He gave the
washcloth a quick toss through the bathroom door and
watched it land on the side of the sink.

Satisfied, he asked, "Think you're ready to go out and
meet Red's most promising grandson?"

"Grandson?"

He nodded. "You'll be amazed at the temperament of
Red's Early Riser, Ronnie. You've never seen two animals more alike. Of course, Riser has a few personality
quirks Red didn't have, but the resemblance is striking."

Veronica smiled. Cole trusted her enough to offer her
a ride on the grandson of Chapman Red. How could she
refuse? And he was speaking to her as if they shared
something much more basic than a mutual love of horses.
As Cole continued to extol Riser's virtues, she marveled
at the warm sense of companionship developing between them.

"A short ride can't hurt," she said confidently. "Let's
go."

The sun was bright and hot on her face, the light breeze
teasing her hair into tangles as Cole lifted her on Early
Riser's saddle and handed her the reins. Veronica felt
sixteen again, healthy and whole, every part of her aching to dig in her heels and let the big horse run.

But the dull twinge of discomfort radiating up through
both her thighs warned her to be cautious, reminding her

she had neither the strength nor the agility to tolerate more than a few minutes in the saddle.

The stallion tossed his head and Veronica reached down to give his sleek red neck a loving pat. Riser moved off at a walk, then pranced sideways, as if impatient with the gentle, yet authoritative hands on the reins.

"Let me know if he's too much for you," Cole called as he walked a few feet to Veronica's left, carrying her crutches, watching for any sign of a problem.

"He's all right," Veronica called back nonchalantly, enjoying the splendid feel of the powerful horse beneath her, savoring the mobility she hadn't felt in the months of lying in bed, limited by weakness and pain. But more than that, riding again—especially the grandson of Chapman Red—gave her a feeling of happiness and contentment deeper than any she'd known for years.

Sensing the short ride to the barn would not be enough for her, Cole walked the horse slowly around the huge two-level barn, then suggested that Veronica ride on her own around one of the smaller paddocks. She gladly consented, but Cole allowed her to complete only two laps in the enclosure before calling her over to him.

"Don't overdo it, Ronnie," he cautioned as she brought the stallion to a halt a few feet from where he stood. He entered the paddock and in seconds had lifted Veronica to the ground, leaving her disappointedly earthbound once again as he handed her the crutches. After removing Riser's saddle and bridle, he ushered Veronica out of the paddock and into the stable. In a few minutes they were walking side by side down the wide aisle of the stable, Cole moving with loose-jointed ease while Veronica made short stilted steps with legs that were only slightly stiffer after her brief ride. But if Veronica was feeling any discomfort from the unaccustomed exercise, her smiling face gave no indication.

Cole was amazed at the transformation in her. Within the past hour, the pale withdrawn young woman with her aura of loneliness had vanished. In her place was a more youthful, animated young woman whose wide smile, healthy flush and sparkling eyes gave her a beautiful warmth and radiance.

She was chattering delightedly to him now, and Cole smiled, suddenly struck by the thought that forgiving Veronica after all these years had liberated this charming young woman. He felt a run of guilt for his harshness eight years before. He couldn't wait to see how she'd react to the second part of his surprise. Touching her arm, he directed her across the aisle to a side door that opened onto another paddock.

Veronica gasped with pleasure when she looked outside, "She's beautiful, Cole," she said as a young sorrel mare trotted over and nudged Cole's arm amicably. He reached up and rubbed the animal's cheek as she automatically nosed Veronica's shoulder then curiously inspected her crutches. "She's not spooked a bit by these."

"Honey Lamb is one of the sweetest-tempered horses I own," Cole explained, then grinned. "We own," he corrected. "She's a little too inquisitive at times, but she's smooth gaited and gentle enough for you to ride until you regain the strength to really handle a spirited horse."

"Oh, Cole." Her bright smile wavered and tears began to flood into her eyes.

"Hey," Cole chided gruffly as he slipped a strong arm around her waist. "If you're going to turn on the sprinklers over every little thing, how am I going to know when I've done something right?" Veronica sniffed back her tears and looked up at him.

"Honey Lamb?"

Cole laughed and his arm tightened briefly. "Jackie named her favorite animals the damnedest things." The wistful look came and went so quickly in Cole's eyes that she almost missed it. Cole glanced down into Veronica's face, his smile coaxing a return of her own. They turned to reenter the barn and were almost to the wide main aisle when Veronica spoke.

"Cole?" The big rancher stopped and cobalt-blue eyes slanted down to meet hers. She was somehow on the verge of both tears and laughter. "Cole, I . . ." A mere thank-you seemed such an inadequate expression for the gratitude she felt. As foolish and impulsive as her next action was, she reached up and placed both hands behind his neck, heedless of the crutches that fell to the floor. Cole allowed his head to be drawn downward by the gentle pressure on his neck, and his hands naturally fell to her waist as he accepted the quick touch of her lips to his.

"Thank you so much, Cole." The kiss had been too light, too gentle. "I can't tell you how much all this means to me." Veronica had unclasped her hands from his neck and they were dropping away when Cole's renewed grip on her waist brought her against him. Veronica's happy smile was startled from her lips as her hands landed gently on his shoulders.

Cole didn't wait to hear the half-formed question on her lips. His mouth descended swiftly, yet settled like a whisper on hers. What started as a simple need for a more satisfying kiss sent a jolt of heat rocketing through his system, surprising him with the unexpected stirring of a depth of passion he'd known only with his wife. But that was long ago, so long ago, Cole realized, and as he took

Ronnie's soft mouth more vigorously, his desire for the woman in his arms became all consuming.

Veronica's had been a child's kiss, a simple sweet expression of gratitude, but the firm pressure of Cole's mouth was mature male. There was an element of wildness in Cole's kiss that she'd never experienced with Eric, a spontaneity that alarmed, yet fascinated.

Before she quite realized it, Veronica was matching Cole's wildness with her own mouth in a fevered attempt to give him a measure of the sensual excitement he was lavishing on her. Somehow she was slipping past rational thought into an unknown area nearing total surrender.

Cole's lips were becoming more insistent, but Veronica was oblivious to the fact that he had lost control or that he was lowering them both onto a bale of hay. His embrace tightened once she was on his lap, and Veronica felt the involuntary melting of her small frame into the hardness of his.

The last remnants of reason called to her, warning her love-drugged mind that something of her essence was being drawn away. The overpowering need to merge with Cole warred against the frightening notion that he was stealing into her very being and extracting the untapped wellspring of love in her heart....

"Dad?"

Veronica floated closer to sanity at the sound of the childish voice. Cole's arms slackened, but he was slow to break off the kiss.

"Dad." Curtis was clearly annoyed.

Sensitive to the impatience a child often feels in the presence of adults who are kissing and embracing, Veronica tried to draw away, embarrassed that Cole kept her firmly in his arms.

"What is it, Curtis?" he asked sternly.

The small boy looked as if he'd forgotten what he'd been about to say. Cole watched his son's obvious discomfort with amused indulgence, but Veronica didn't like the resentment building in those large gray eyes. She liked it even less when his gaze moved over her and noted that she was sitting on his father's lap, held there securely in his father's oaklike arms. There was no mistaking the tiny glimmers of anger that darted into those solemn gray eyes, or the companion tightening of the small mouth.

"You promised to take me for ice cream," he said sulkily, his tone of voice bringing a frown of displeasure to his father's face.

"I said I might," Cole corrected patiently. "Your timing leaves something to be desired, son. Haven't we talked about interrupting?"

Curtis blushed, embarrassed. "You weren't talking to her," Curtis told his father reasonably.

Veronica might have found Curtis's reply amusing, but the hurt in the boy's expression tugged at her heart. The slim fingers that rested behind Cole's head jerked warningly on a thick black lock. In response, a wide smile spread across Cole's face. Curtis seemed to relax at the sight.

"You've got me there, Curt," Cole admitted. "What do you say the three of us climb into the pickup and go for ice cream? I heard they're having a special on hot-fudge sundaes." Curtis's quick grin dissolved. Instantly, Veronica sensed she was the reason.

"What do you say we leave me at home?" Veronica suggested, allowing her tiredness to show. "I'm afraid I've overdone things a little today. Would you mind handing me my crutches, Curtis?"

The boy was quick to comply, but the unfriendly look in his eyes told her clearly that his eagerness had more to do with getting her away from his father than giving his assistance. Veronica thanked Curtis and he ran out to the truck.

"Are you really tired, or are you trying to do an imitation of a small kitchen appliance?" Cole's question referred to her offer not to court Curtis's friendship if Cole kept him home more, assuring him Curtis would likely pay her no more notice than he would an appliance or a piece of furniture.

"Both." Veronica got to her feet. Now that she wasn't touching Cole, now that the delayed sense of weariness was asserting itself on her tired body, Veronica was sobering rapidly from the euphoria of the afternoon. One glance at Cole's iron expression as he fell into step beside her thrust her back into all the old familiar insecurities. So he had forgiven her, taken her riding, then offered her the use of a lovely mare. And her foolish little kiss had triggered his sensual appetite. He'd said before that it had been a while since he'd been with a woman....

A cold sick feeling of shame and fear rushed up inside her. She remembered how she'd felt after the kiss she and Cole had shared when she'd bandaged his hand. She couldn't be intimate with a man—ever. The scars from her accident were too repulsive.

Veronica glanced at Cole again. What a superb virile male specimen he was, with a sexual confidence and experience that warned her he was accustomed to much more from a woman than kisses.

"I hope the ride won't make you too sore," Cole said. "Should I get out the liniment later and give you a rubdown after Curtis and I get back?" His intimate tone as they reached the porch steps sent a jolt of apprehension through her—magnifying her fear of what such physical closeness would reveal to him. No man could stand the sight of her scars—Eric's abandonment was proof of that.

Veronica stepped onto the porch, then turned to face Cole. "Look. I think it would be wise to keep our relationship with each other as businesslike as possible while I'm here. I'm not going to be here long, so there's no sense in flirting with complications." A wry smile twisted her lips, stilling their trembling. "We've shared a couple of hot little kisses, but I think we both recognize a mistake when we see one."

Cole's expression grew so thunderous she almost faltered.

"And poor Curtis!" She went on. "We've managed to make him feel threatened and unhappy."

Cole's jaw muscles flexed ominously and Veronica took that as her cue to be silent. "Have fun at the Dairy Queen." Veronica turned and moved through the porch door, leaving Cole staring after her for a moment before he turned to join his son.

CHAPTER SIX

"What's that stuff?"

Veronica smiled tolerantly at the boy who stood by her elbow. Now that Curtis was eating breakfast and supper at the house and generally spending much more time at home, the relative calm of her couple of weeks at the ranch had vanished. Veronica didn't mind Curtis's rambunctiousness, but the fact that he seemed determined to make things harder on her had proven to be more emotionally wearing than she'd have thought possible. It gave her a whole new perspective on the problems she had caused her mother's suitors.

"It's called Christmas Stew."

His nose wrinkled into an expression of disgust that was becoming all too familiar to her. "Christmas Stew! I hate stew."

"You might like this stew. Can you guess why it's called Christmas Stew?" Her smile was open, friendly.

"I don't know." And the scowl on his handsome little face told her he didn't care to know. Patiently Veronica continued talking.

"It's called Christmas Stew because most of the ingredients are either red or green, like Christmas decorations."

"That part ain't," he challenged as he pointed to a piece of meat. Veronica glanced down at the triumphant look on his face and knew Curtis was only interested in the stew now because he'd found something to be disagreeable about.

She resisted the temptation to correct his grammar and said, "There's one other ingredient in there that's not red or green." She wondered if he'd spied the diced onion that had been cooked almost transparent.

"Where?"

Veronica lifted the wide wooden spoon from the rim of the simmering pot and deftly skimmed off a few bits for Curtis to see.

"What's that?" he asked suspiciously.

"Onion."

"I hate onion, too."

Veronica laughed. "You're going to be in sad shape come supper," she kidded. "But you'll at least give the stew a fair tasting, won't you?" Curtis's expression was pure mutiny.

"I don't like that rule," he scowled, referring to Veronica's requirement that he at least taste a new food before he rejected it.

"I'm sorry, Curtis, but the only way you can find out what you like or don't like is by tasting," she told him patiently.

"If you were as good a cook as my Aunt Helen, I'd like everything you cook." Veronica refused to be either surprised or rankled by the childish jibe. With a thoughtful expression on her face, she glanced down at Curtis's glum face.

"Would you like me to ask Helen for some of your favorite recipes? There's no reason I can't make some of the foods you like best." Veronica's smile was meant to be encouraging, but Curtis only managed to look more annoyed.

"I don't like the way you cook." And with that final pronouncement disappeared out through the porch door.

Veronica pondered for a moment, then checked her watch before crossing the floor to another cupboard. Opening the door, she selected enough boxes of chocolate instant pudding to fill eight parfait glasses.

"He'll probably find something wrong with that idea, too." Cole's voice startled her. Guiltily she glanced over her shoulder at him, then disheartened, she started to put the boxes away.

"Go ahead and make some up if you want to, Ronnie. If he complains, I'll split his share with you." Cole walked to the refrigerator for a glass of iced tea.

Both Chapman males had been hard to get along with all week. Since Sunday, Cole had been cool and uncommunicative. Veronica had spent nearly every moment she wasn't preparing meals, or taking her daily exercise, working on the small baby quilt she'd started—contributing her part to the distancing between them by avoiding Cole altogether. She had begun riding Honey Lamb every day, but Cole didn't once offer to go with her, instead leaving the task of saddling the mare or accompanying her to Shorty or one of the other men.

"I'm giving you the day off tomorrow, Veronica."

Veronica looked at Cole, who was leaning against the counter nearby while he drank his tea.

"There's a woman coming out in the morning to cook breakfast and I thought she might as well give us a full day. Her references indicate she's pretty good in the kitchen, so she could be the one to replace you." Cole's face was absolutely unreadable, his eyes betraying nothing but a casual interest in her reaction.

Veronica summoned up a smile from the surprise she felt, then turned back to the mixing bowl and began tearing open pudding boxes. "I wish you luck," she told him, moving toward the refrigerator for milk. Stronger now, she managed very well on one crutch while she carried the milk jug to where she was working.

"Which day will we count as the first in the week's notice you're giving me? Tomorrow?" Veronica measured out the milk while she talked.

"I haven't hired her yet," Cole reminded her gruffly.

"Oh, you will," she said, then smiled, certain Cole wouldn't know that her amused expression hid the hurt she felt. "Curtis is getting pretty tired of corn flakes and peanut-butter sandwiches." Veronica switched on the mixer to discourage further conversation.

With the end of her stay in sight, she felt nothing but disappointment. As Cole left the room she chided herself. Things between her and Cole had improved more than she'd ever imagined they would. Just because they were avoiding each other now was no reason to feel disappointed. They would part on friendly terms and Cole would surely remember her the way she was now—older, more mature, useful. At least if they happened to meet in the future, there would be no hostile exchanges like the ones they'd had when she first came back to Wyoming.

Yet when Veronica poured the thickening pudding into the parfait glasses, she felt a prickle of tears. Scolding herself for being such a sentimental sap, she finished up in the kitchen and left the house for a walk.

THE EVENING HAD BEEN LONELY. Veronica had gone to her room after cleaning up the supper dishes. She'd spent a long time soaking in the tub before she put on her nightgown. She had just finished drying her hair when she heard a knock, then Cole's voice at her door. Hastily grabbing her robe, she belted it around herself and called for him to come in.

Veronica was seated before the dresser mirror brushing out tangles as he crossed the room and stood behind her. Their eyes met in the glass with an impact that brought a rush of excitement into her system. Even now that she was sure her stay was limited only to a few more days, she couldn't help the secret longing she felt—a longing more than just to stay.

Yet that longing was as futile as it was unwelcome. She had looked at Jackie's picture only the day before and had been reminded of what a beautiful woman she had been. After being married to someone like Jackie, Cole would never be content with anyone less, and certainly not his former stepsister. Although the past had been virtually resolved between them, Veronica felt herself no match for the sweet memories Cole would certainly have of the mother of his only child—a child who resented Veronica's presence.

"There are one or two things I'd like to take up with you, Veronica." Cole had her instant attention when he spoke to her in that tone, dropping the use of the nickname his father had bestowed upon her. Veronica waited, expecting him to go on, but he merely stood there, silent.

"Well?" she prompted, uncomfortable with the way his eyes were starting to stray over her reflection. The obvious preoccupation he seemed to have with the way her light robe was draped over her small breasts signaled her to beware. Had her earlier fears been correct? Had Cole been without a woman for so long that he'd developed an interest in her because she was convenient?

Fully aware of how vulnerable she was to any demonstration of affection from Cole, she was anxious for him to say what he had in mind and leave her room.

"Since I gave you tomorrow off, I was wondering if you'd have dinner with me tomorrow night." Cole's deep voice was like rough silk, a caress of her senses. Resisting its drawling persuasion was almost a physical pain, but Veronica didn't hesitate.

"No, I don't think so, Cole. Besides, don't you want to taste the new woman's cooking?

"I'll be there to sample breakfast and lunch. The boys will give me a report on dinner. After all, it's them she's cooking for."

She ran the brush briskly through her thick brown hair for several strokes before finding her hand captured in the firm warmth of Cole's. Violet eyes found his again in the mirror.

"So why not come?" His look was shrewd, almost calculating. Veronica tugged her hand free.

"Don't tell me you're so accustomed to having women fall all over you for a dinner date that you give the third degree to the rare one who declines," she kidded, hoping to deflect his question. One corner of Cole's mouth lifted in mild amusement.

"I think I know what you're trying to do, Ronnie."

"I'm relieved," she parried, smiling brightly to cover the trapped feeling that engulfed her suddenly. "I was beginning to think you weren't going to take no for an answer." Veronica started to rise when Cole's hands settled over her shoulders, their pressure just enough to keep her seated.

"You're tense, Ronnie," he said, as his fingers began probing her taut muscles. The warmth of his touch was sending an almost unendurable heat through her system.

"Thanks, Cole," she said hurriedly, raising her hands to brush away his gentle grip. "It's much better now."

Stubbornly he maintained his hold.

"The country air has done you good, Ronnie." Cole's husky voice was a sensual accompaniment to the feel of his hands and the heat that radiated from the strong muscular body just behind her. "I can't get over the change in you in only three weeks."

Veronica felt a rush of panic. Cole had asked her once before if it had been a long time since she'd been with a man. It was clear to her from his invitation to dinner, his flattery, and his seductive ministrations, that he was about to hint at the mutual release he thought they were both seeking. The fact that she'd likely be leaving very soon permitted Cole to indulge in an affair that would be brief and remain discreet.

"Relax," he coaxed softly as his hands worked a bit harder to disburse the increasing tension in her shoulders, his eyes never leaving her face. "And say yes about tomorrow night."

"Why?" she challenged, determined to resist the slow seduction of her will. Cole's brows rose at her tone.

"I'd like to be with you in a relaxed atmosphere where we're served good food that you don't have to tire yourself preparing." Cole's hands worked toward her neck, then paused to comb tenderly through her silken hair. "And I'd like to get to know you better."

The hot and cold shivers of pleasure caused by the teasing involvement of his fingers in her hair changed into a blazing resentment that brought her to her feet with surprising speed.

"What a clever line," she snapped, rounding on him. "Now that I'll be leaving soon, you suddenly want to get to know me better. I suppose you think I'll be so flattered I won't remember how determined you've been to avoid me all week. I might be a little susceptible to a man who knows how to push all the right buttons," she ranted, unable to hold back the anger that had simmered in the months since Eric's departure, "but experience has destroyed any illusions I might have had about men and what really motivates their interest in me." Veronica halted, then rushed on recklessly.

"If you're looking for some desperate female to relieve your male frustrations, you'd better look someplace else. You're about six months too late with this one." Cole's eyes narrowed and Veronica suddenly realized her uncontrollable outburst had revealed too much.

"Careful," Cole cautioned as he braved the temper in her violet eyes. "I think you're jumping to conclusions." Heat shot into her cheeks as her anger faltered and chagrin mingled painfully with her roiling emotions. "Just because your divorce has left you feeling wary of men, don't assume that every man who finds himself attracted to you is only looking for a release of sexual tension." Cole paused. "And I'm not in the habit of bestowing my attentions on a woman because of a warped sense of generosity. I don't feel sorry enough for any woman to take her to bed." Silence fell and left a painful awkwardness between them.

"And while we're on the subject, how long did it take for this prize-winning husband of yours to leave you with such dismal expectations of men and their motives?"

Veronica couldn't look at Cole. Fumbling fingers reached for the crutches leaning against the wall. "I don't want to talk about it," she murmured as she moved past him in as much of a retreat as she could manage.

"Maybe you'd be better off if you did," Cole suggested, his tone mellowing from harshness to a velvet rasp.

Veronica didn't comment; she'd said too much already. Strange how until her angry outburst a few moments earlier she'd only been able to feel hurt and humiliation over Eric's defection. But however strong her delayed anger had been, her charge hadn't been fair to Cole.

"I'm sorry about that little tirade, Cole. It was uncalled for. I guess I have developed a pretty negative attitude in some areas."

"You could take the first dose of cure for that negative attitude by changing your mind about tomorrow night." Cole moved closer, but didn't touch her. He didn't have to. His gentle tenacity was persuading her.

"All right," she murmured, sadly realizing she wasn't strong enough to resist what could be one of her few opportunities to be with Cole before she walked out of his life forever. "I'll go with you tomorrow night."

DESPITE ALL HER BEST EFFORTS, Veronica was behaving like a teenager on her first date. She fussed over her appearance for almost two hours before she was satisfied with her makeup and her shoulder-length page-boy hairstyle. She used gold combs to draw the hair on each side of her head into soft upsweeps that accented her high cheekbones.

She found the ride into Cheyenne slightly unnerving, as she recalled being in the passenger seat with Eric driving and the awful results. Yet as if Cole was aware of her silent torment, he did his best to distract her with conversation.

Of course, Cole was a powerful distraction, and no more so than tonight in the navy slacks that encased his lean hips and muscular thighs, and the sky-blue silk shirt with the elaborately embroidered yoke that intensified the blue of his eyes. The western-cut jacket and the black dress Stetson completed the casual look of a rancher going to town on a Saturday night.

Veronica nervously adjusted a lapel of her ivory jacket, which matched her linen slacks. She'd chosen the indigo blouse beneath the jacket for the way its color flattered her violet eyes, not realizing until she'd seen Cole what a pleasing harmony of color the two of them created with their choices of blue and ivory.

Once they were seated next to each other in the lounge of the newly opened Western Club, Veronica enjoyed the warm ambience. The booth Cole had chosen for them while they waited for a table in the dining room was upholstered in a saddle-blanket weave with carved leather insets that continued the western theme of the restaurant and lounge.

"Are you as nervous a driver as you seem to be a passenger?" Cole asked her after he'd ordered drinks. The question reminded her that she'd always found some excuse to drive herself into town, even when she and Cole were going to buy groceries together.

"No. I guess it still bothers me to ride in the passenger seat," she answered without thinking. "I had to keep reminding myself that you were so—" Veronica's face paled at what she'd almost said. Sober. Cole was sober, she'd reminded herself over and over. Eric had been drunk.

"Your mother said your accident was caused by a drunk driver," Cole probed, and Veronica was uncomfortable with the sudden interest in his eyes. The waitress came and smilingly placed their drinks in front of them, but she departed too quickly for Veronica to manage a smooth change of subject.

With a sigh she said frankly, "I was involved in one of the most preventable of drunk-driver accidents—if there is such a thing. I was sober, but I let a drunk climb behind the wheel and drive because I..." Veronica hesitated, knowing her confession would take Cole a step closer to knowing what really happened to her marriage. "Because I didn't want to risk an argument." Perhaps it was time to allow her humiliation to be aired. She had carried it so long now that she was growing more and more weary of trying to conceal it from those who didn't already know about it. Besides, all of her friends and half of New York knew the story.

Yet still she held back the entire truth. "We'd just been to a beautiful wedding and then attended the reception. It had been a perfect day I didn't want to provoke a scene," Veronica explained, listening to the recounting of the story as if it were being told by someone else. "All our friends were there, all Eric's relatives, even the press. I can remember thinking that it was only a few blocks to our hotel and the traffic was about as slow as it was going to get for New York. I made the near-fatal mistake of assuming that accidents only happen to other people. Thank God it was a one-car accident and no pedestrians were involved!"

"What happened to the driver?" Cole asked when she paused for several moments.

Veronica forced her eyes to meet Cole's as she continued, "He passed out before impact and bruised his forehead on the steering wheel. My corner of the car hit a brick building and I didn't fare nearly as well," she admitted in an attempt at light understatement. In fact she'd almost bled to death before rescue workers could free her from the wreckage.

"This driver," Cole persisted, his expression changing from repressed anger to a look of dawning realization, "was he your husband?"

Veronica's gaze lowered to the glass she'd been twisting nervously on the cocktail napkin. "Yes." She still found herself unable to tell Cole that the wedding they'd just come from had been her wedding. Or that Eric had been shocked and sickened by the swollen black-and-blue mask that had once been his bride's face, and the battered broken body swathed in plaster and bandages. So much so that when the doctors gave Eric their initial grim prognosis for her recovery, he'd fled from the hospital— and by the time she regained consciousness several days later, he'd fled from her life. She learned from her mother later that he'd already consulted a lawyer about an annulment.

A strong tanned hand reached for the slim one in her lap and gave it a consoling squeeze. Veronica forced a smile and looked up into the eyes of the man who sat next to her in the booth. She saw sympathy there, but not pity. Thank God she didn't see pity. That she couldn't have stood. Still, she wasn't ready to tell Cole the rest of it. Not yet. Besides, what she'd told him already threatened to put a pall of gloom over the entire evening and she didn't want that. Not with Cole.

"What about the new cook, Mrs. Engstrom?" Veronica asked, changing the unhappy direction the conversation had taken. "Do you think you're going to hire her?" The thought of the cook's eccentricities made Veronica's eyes twinkle with amusement, and she had to bite her lip to keep from smiling.

Cole's brows went up as he shook his head. "I've rarely heard a man cuss the way that woman did today. She was a good cook, but I heard words come out of that mouth that'd scald the hair off a dog. It's a wonder the smoke detectors didn't go off."

Veronica wasn't able to hold back any longer, and she dissolved into laughter, "I thought Teddy and Jim were going to faint from embarrassment," she gasped when she was able to control her mirth. "And Shorty! His face went so red it was nearly purple!"

"It was probably all that blue air that made it look purple," Cole added, joining Veronica in her laughter. Their joking went on for several minutes—until the moment Cole happened to glance toward the door. The change that came over his happy relaxed expression prompted Veronica to look in the same direction.

Helen and her husband, Bob, stood in the doorway to the lounge with Jessica Ryan and a man Veronica recognized as Wylie Edwards, a local rancher. Helen and Jessie seemed to spy Cole and Veronica at the same time, and there was no mistaking the subject of the conspiratorial whispering between the two women. Helen guided Bob in their direction just long enough for him to see Cole and think it was his idea to stop by their table to say hello.

Veronica glanced sideways at Cole to see if he had interpreted Helen's maneuvering the way she had, but he seemed to be taking a lot of belated interest in his drink. When Veronica looked again at the approaching couples and saw the possessive way Wylie Edwards had hooked his arm around Jessie's waist, she realized what had prompted Cole's quick change. He was jealous.

CHAPTER SEVEN

"BY GOLLY, COLE," Bob was saying in his typical fashion as he grasped Cole's hand and pumped it firmly. "What are you doin' in a place like this when you got Veronica cookin' for you at home?" Veronica blushed at the compliment from one of her most recent admirers. Bob had been over at noon one day and had left raving about the delicious casserole she'd prepared.

"If I don't give her a night off once in a while, I might find myself doing my own cooking again," Cole joked back before he greeted Helen and Jessie. His nod to Wylie was cool.

"Say, it isn't often we're all together like this," Helen piped up, beaming at the group. "Do you mind if we join you?"

Put that way, how could she and Cole refuse, Veronica thought sourly. Both couples slid into the horseshoe-shaped booth, crowding Veronica and Cole closer together physically, but driving them apart in every other way, as the conversation around the table centered on topics that excluded Veronica. They'd been sitting there only a few moments before Helen made a second suggestion—that they all change their table reservations in the dining room to avoid dividing the happy group.

Jessie echoed Helen's suggestion, and in an instant Veronica and Cole had become part of a party of six. Veronica felt much of the evening's pleasure fade. Even if Cole had wanted to, there was no polite way for him to refuse.

It was clear to Veronica that happy-go-lucky Bob was oblivious to his wife's impromptu scheme. Besides, he seemed to thoroughly enjoy the fun and companionship of a group, the bigger the better. Poor Wylie was looking at Jessie as if he'd walk over hot coals for her, while Cole, sipping his drink, appeared to have temporarily withdrawn into himself. Veronica became convinced that he wished he'd asked Jessie out instead.

So she kept a polite silence, toying with the swizzle stick in her drink, listening to the happy conversation, yet feeling as distinctly separate from this group of old friends as if she'd been seated at the next table. And when they were ushered into the dining room, Veronica felt even more dismal when Jessie was seated on the other side of Cole.

Despite what Veronica expected, Cole made certain she was included, deliberately drawing her into the conversation. Their decision to order the dinner for two—they both found the roast tenderloin of beef with Madeira sauce appealing—enabled them to be involved with each other much more closely than if they'd each chosen something different.

And from the dagger looks Jessie gave her, Veronica was certain neither she nor Helen cared for the fact that for dessert Cole ordered one piece of the disgustingly rich chocolate fudge cheesecake with the understanding that Veronica share it with him.

"I admire a man who knows when to pull away from the table," Bob commented, a mischievous twinkle in his eyes. "Since you and Veronica have been dividin' everything tonight, I reckon you've noticed her cookin' is startin' to put a little weather boarding around your middle." Cole looked anything but amused as he drew open his jacket to glance at his stomach. When he looked up, his sheepish grin brought a chorus of laughter.

"Speaking of cooking," Helen put in, "when does that woman you had come in today start working for you, Cole?"

Cole grimaced and Veronica watched his profile with amusement as he explained Mrs. Engstrom's colorful dialect. Neither Helen nor Jessie concealed their disappointment very successfully when Cole told them in no uncertain terms that he wouldn't consider hiring the woman.

"If I could clone Ronnie, I'd have just what I'm looking for," Cole told his friends, and Veronica flushed with pleasure at his outspoken praise. Cole raised his arm then and settled it warmly over her shoulders. He didn't remove it until dessert arrived.

After dinner the group migrated back to a table in the bar that looked out over the dance floor. Jessie and Helen excused themselves and went off in search of the ladies room. A few moments later, Veronica decided to follow, making her way carefully with her crutches through the evening crowd. The door to the ladies room had just swished closed behind her when she heard Helen's voice.

"I certainly wouldn't let it upset me, Jess," she was saying. "Besides, you can't possibly think that Cole honestly prefers Veronica to you. Look at her."

Veronica had heard enough. She had just turned to make a quiet retreat when Jessie spoke.

"So you think this is just a mercy date?" Jessie asked.

"What else could it be? About all she can really do is cook. She doesn't even have much of a personality."

Stunned at the cruel words, Veronica stepped into the small sitting room area just outside. Was she really only a "mercy date"? Getting a firm grip on herself, she reentered the rest room noisily, making sure her presence was noticed. There was absolute silence as she repaired her makeup and ran a brush quickly through her hair. After Helen and Jessie left, Veronica waited a few moments before heading back, determined to forget what she'd just heard.

"Come on, Cole." Jessie was saying, her perfect lips set in an appealing pout as she tugged on Cole's arm. "Dance with me. You know how I love to dance to fast numbers."

Bob and Helen were already on the dance floor, and Bob was swinging Helen around with more enthusiasm than grace. Wylie danced only to slow music, and this gave Jessie the opportunity to pursue Cole.

"Go ahead," Veronica said at his questioning glance, forcing a smile to let him know she didn't mind. But she did. It had been a long time since she'd danced and she suddenly wanted more than anything to have the grace and freedom to be able to get on a dance floor. She wanted to dance even more as she watched Cole go off with Jessie, joining the thickening crowd of dancers.

Sullen and in obvious bad temper, Wylie ordered a double vodka, which he drank broodingly as he watched his date dance with Cole. When Jessie persuaded Cole to stay with her for a second number, Wylie moved into the chair next to Veronica.

"Now that she's got him, this is what it will be like the rest of the night," he predicted glumly.

"Surely not," Veronica said with far more confidence than she felt. Although she knew that Cole wouldn't abandon her for the evening, she couldn't say the same for Jessie's sense of fairness. There was no doubt in her mind that Jessie could easily arrive with one man and spend all her time with another without feeling the slightest twinge of conscience.

"Damn!" Wylie's voice could be heard in the lull between songs. When the band started a new number, a slow one this time, Wylie grew even angrier. "Look at them," he said, nodding toward Cole and Jessie. "They aren't going to stop till morning." Wylie downed the rest of his drink in one gulp and motioned to the waitress to bring another.

Veronica knew that with Wylie it was the booze talking, but as she watched Cole and Jessie together on the dance floor, she had difficulty fighting her own jealousy. They looked perfect together. Jessie's voluptuous body was pressed sensually against the lean hardness of Cole's, her blond cover-girl looks providing the perfect complement to Cole's rugged dark handsomeness.

Suddenly, Veronica found herself wishing Cole would hire Mrs. Engstrom. If he did, she'd be leaving in a day or so, before these hopeless feelings grew into something with a far greater potential to destroy her. *I barely survived what Eric did,* she thought, *and if I fall in love with Cole, how will I recover from that?* It came as a shock to realize that the emotion Cole aroused in her was far more intense than what she'd felt for Eric. But her shock was even greater as she realized she was already deeply in love with Cole.

How had it happened? How could she have blundered into something as dangerous as falling in love with Cole after the way she'd been hurt by Eric?

"Nothing keeps that woman from chasing Cole," she heard Wylie grouse. "If she ever got any real competition for him, she might get discouraged and give up."

Wylie took another drink. "Hell." Wylie's glass hit the table top with a thud. "I'm not gonna just sit here like some mongrel dog and wait for her to come back to the table. I spent too damned much money on her tonight to put up with this." Wylie turned his head and stared at Veronica with drunken intensity for a moment. "You want me to drive you home?"

The color fled from her cheeks at the very thought of getting into a car with anyone in Wylie's condition.

"They've only danced a couple of dances together," she said reasonably. "Let's give them a little more time." Wylie lurched back in his chair and his anger seemed to subside, but Veronica realized his dark mood was affecting her. She was beginning to feel as jilted and unwelcome as he did, perhaps more.

As she studied Wylie's profile, she decided that this hazel-eyed young man with sun-streaked brown hair was more than marginally attractive. He and Jessie would make a nice-looking couple, but it was plain that Wylie felt far more for the beautiful Jessie than she felt for him. Veronica understood his hurt and disappointment all too well.

When the song ended, Cole and Jessie made their way back to the table while Bob and Helen remained on the dance floor for the slow tune that followed. Jessie took her seat next to Wylie, a sense of obligation in her sulking manner. Veronica watched her and Wylie together, amazed at how their less-than-cheerful dispositions made them well suited to each other.

As Veronica sipped her drink, she felt awkward knowing that Cole had probably returned to the table out of consideration for her and Wylie rather than out of genuine desire to be with her. He and Jessie had surely been having a much better time with each other than they could expect to have with their respective dates.

Cole was still standing. He touched Veronica's shoulder, and she turned her head, her gaze traveling up his long lean body to the darkly handsome face smiling down at her. The evening was over. The thought had her fumbling for her purse.

"You don't need your purse to dance," Cole said as he removed the purse strap from her fingers.

"But I can't dance," she said.

"Yes you can," he said smiling. "I'll help you."

Feeling uncoordinated and more than a little embarrassed, she reached for her crutches.

"You don't need them," he said as he helped her up and assisted her to the edge of the dance floor. Moments later, she was in his arms, moving stiffly in contrast to his masculine grace. Cole led with a small stepping pattern to accommodate her, and even though their embrace gave her legs all the support she needed, Veronica was all too aware of her awkwardness.

"Relax," Cole growled. "Don't worry about winning any dance contests. Just listen to the music and let your body do what it feels." Veronica looked up into his face and was drawn to the intensity of his gaze. Violet eyes registered the unmistakable change that came into Cole's as the darker blue deepened, their pupils widening until only a tiny rim of color surrounded the blackness.

She was dimly aware of the softness and gradual pliancy of her body against Cole's hard thighs. The strength of the large frame she was pressed ever tighter against sent her into a near-hypnotic state of arousal. Cole moved to the rhythm of the music whether she faltered or not and the very constancy of his movements suffused her body with sensual heat and made her weak with wanting. She hardly noticed when one slow song melded into the next. She was aware only of the power and male vigor of the body that guided her, supported her and subtly brought her femininity to life.

Cole's arms tightened until she was against him fully, her cheek pressed against his broad chest. Her eyes were just drifting closed blissfully, inhaling Cole's warmth and scent of after-shave, when she caught sight of Wylie and Jessie on the dance floor.

The venomous look Jessie gave her over Wylie's shoulder was chilling, sobering, snapping Veronica from her daze of sensuality. For Jessie's displeasure, Veronica knew, could have unpleasant consequences. More than once in the time Veronica spent at the ranch years earlier, she had unwittingly been maneuvered and victimized by Jessie's vengeance. Jessie and Wylie disappeared from view when Cole angled their steps in a new direction.

"You and Jessie still have it in for each other, don't you?" Cole's question was more a statement of fact than a question, and Veronica pulled away slightly to look up into his frowning expression.

"I don't have it in for Jessie," Veronica said.

Cole's face hardened and his eyes shifted away from hers.

"Jessie denied it, too."

"Well, Jessie is—" Veronica stopped her angry exclamation, frustrated that she couldn't be candid about Jessie without sounding vindictive.

"Lying?" Cole supplied for her, the smirk on his lips conveying his skepticism.

Just like before, Veronica thought, astonished at the old feeling of helplessness. Cole had never been able to see through Jessie's perfidy. Veronica abruptly stopped dancing, and made a move to leave the floor.

Cole's hands clamped like steel around her narrow waist. "You're really worked up, aren't you?" His eyes narrowed with faint incredulity on Veronica's flushed face. Violet eyes that sparkled with anger stared back steadily, defiantly.

"Yes, I'm angry," she said as calmly as her quivering voice would allow. "Jessie could tell you the earth was flat and you'd believe it." Veronica was unaware of the sudden glint of perception in Cole's expression. Her eyes shied guiltily from his and her slim fingers tightened on the thickly muscled forearms beneath her hands.

"I'm sorry," she murmured contritely. "You love Jessie and I shouldn't have said anything against her. Please don't let anything I've said color your relationship with her." Veronica again tried to move away, her eyes veering apprehensively to his when he didn't release her.

"Would you stay and dance with me some more?" Cole asked as the band began another slow tune. The inviting smile on his face brought an uncertain curve to her lips.

"You aren't angry with me?" Now it was Veronica's turn to look surprised.

"I wasn't angry in the first place," Cole rumbled softly, as he pulled her close and began to lead her gently in the dance.

But as Veronica relaxed in his arms and felt her senses succumb to Cole's nearness, she knew they were both less than pleased with the way the evening had turned out.

CHAPTER EIGHT

"YOU DON'T WANT CURTIS to have any fun, do you?" Jessie hissed at Veronica, berating her for her cautiousness.

The two young women were standing in the yard between the house and the driveway, one wearing soiled garden gloves and old clothes with grass stains on the knees, the other dressed in a bright red halter top and designer jeans, her sunglasses parked on top of her lush golden head. Curtis stood in the back of Jessie's green pickup watching the two argue, the mutiny on his young face a clear indication of who championed his cause.

"I mean it, Jessie," Veronica insisted. "I won't let you take Curtis without Cole's permission, and even with it he'd have to be buckled into a seat belt inside the cab of that pickup."

"What gives you the right to say what Curtis does or doesn't do?" the blonde challenged.

"Cole left Curtis with me for the morning. He's not going anywhere without Cole's permission, and when he gives it I'm going to suggest that allowing you to give Curtis a wild ride into town in the back of that truck is dangerous."

"My God, Veronica. Curtis has ridden all over this ranch in the back of pickups from the time he could walk." Jessie's arm swung in a belligerent arc.

"That may be, Jessie, but I doubt very much that anyone around here pulls stunts like you did just coming in here. If you had wanted to convince me that you're a responsible driver, you shouldn't have fishtailed the last quarter mile then slammed on the brakes just in time to miss my car by a hair's breadth."

"I know what I'm doing, Ronnie," Jessie insisted. "I'm in control of that truck every moment."

"And that's what makes you such a dangerous driver—you think you're in control. You've been trusting a lot to luck and I won't let you take chances with the boy's life." Veronica was immovable on the subject. She had spent enough time in hospitals and rehabilitation centers to have seen and heard several horror stories, most of the heartbreakingly tragic ones concerning children who had become tiny projectiles in relatively minor accidents because they were not properly restrained in car safety seats or seat belts.

"Oh, I get it." Now the amber eyes were narrowed, speculative. "You really are after Cole, aren't you? You must think that keeping Curtis from spending time with me will cut me off from both of them."

Veronica was distressed at Jessie's words. Furthermore she was sure that Curtis could hear every word—whatever Jessie's faults, Veronica knew the boy idolized the woman.

"I am not 'after' Cole," Veronica said quietly, struggling to keep her agitation under control. "And I have no objection to you taking Curtis anywhere—if you get Cole's permission first and see that Curtis wears a seat belt while he's in the truck with you."

"But I've had Curtis ride with me a hundred times and he's never gotten so much as a scratch," Jessie said dismissively. "All you have to do is tell Cole when he comes to the house that I've taken Curtis into Cheyenne for the day. He won't mind." Jessie turned away and strode toward her truck. Curtis's face broke into a big smile as he obviously assumed Jessie had got her way.

"Jessie!" Veronica moved swiftly on her crutches after her, desperate to keep Jessie from undermining her authority and endangering Curtis. *If anything happens to that boy while he is in my care...* Veronica was terrified at the thought. "Wait Jessie! You can't just drive off with the boy."

But Jessie ignored her and was striding around the truck to the driver's side when Veronica reached the passenger door. Quickened by frustration and concern, Veronica jerked the door open and climbed in far enough to pull the keys from the ignition. She had just closed the door and slipped the keys into her jeans pocket when Jessie came around the truck to confront her.

"That was a childish thing to do, Veronica!"

"Childish or not, you're going to get Cole's permission first." Veronica's eyes shifted from Jessie's furious face to Curtis's scowl. "Come on, Curtis. Let's go find your father." Veronica turned to head in the direction of the barns, then froze when she saw Cole's iron expression as he stood watching from the corner of the house.

"What's going on here?" Cole's gaze slid from Jessie to Veronica, his look seeming to lay the blame equally between them. "You can give Jessie back her keys."

Veronica felt her face warm as she realized Cole had seen how she'd come to have Jessie's keys in her pocket. Removing her glove, she dug into her jeans and handed them to a triumphant Jessie.

"I told you, didn't I?" Jessie said to Veronica, giving Cole a knowing look that made Veronica feel small.

"Come down out of the truck, Curtis," Cole said. "You're not going anywhere."

Suddenly Jessie didn't look so triumphant as Curtis reluctantly obeyed, but began whining to know why.

"Go to your room, son. I'll be in to explain why in a little while." Curtis's lower lip was trembling and Veronica's heart went out to him. When Curtis went inside, Cole moved closer to Veronica and Jessie.

"I don't want Curtis witnessing anything like this again." Cole's stern look included them both. "Jessie, Curtis was Veronica's responsibility, and from now on I expect you to abide by her decisions without passing judgment on them in front of Curtis. And I don't want you to make any remarks to him later, either," Cole added before his voice went less stern. "I'd appreciate it if you'd forget about taking Curtis today. Maybe one day next week you can stop by."

Jessie looked stricken. "But Cole—"

"Please, Jessie." Cole's voice was gentle, regretful, and Jessie seemed to brighten. Flashing Veronica a satisfied look, Jessie strode off with her usual easy grace and climbed into the pickup. The smirk that marred her perfect mouth told Veronica whom the woman believed would bear the brunt of Cole's displeasure. When the green pickup roared out of earshot, Veronica faced Cole.

"I'm not sorry, Cole," she told him firmly. "And I was going to insist that you not allow Curtis to go with her even if she did agree to buckle him in a seat belt. She's just too reckless."

"I saw the way she drove up," Cole said grimly, his eyes running over Veronica's defiant look.

"I think it would be a good idea if you kept Curtis with you when he's home," she said. "I can't guarantee he won't be in the middle of something just as unpleasant in the future." She took a steadying breath. "And I just don't want the responsibility of taking care of him." Besides, she thought bleakly, Curtis resented her presence and would barely heed anything she said.

"If that's the way you feel." Cole let his voice trail off, his jaw flexing with what she thought was ill-concealed displeasure. "But I think you ought to know that there's no doubt in my mind that you have Curtis's safety and best interests at heart. After what I just saw, I trust you completely with my son."

Veronica frowned in confusion. "But I handled it all wrong." She was thinking of the way she'd grabbed Jessie's keys and stuffed them into her pocket when she couldn't think of a more mature way to handle the situation.

"Jessie didn't exactly leave you with many polite options," Cole acknowledged, then paused. "I'm sorry, Ronnie. I didn't realize how spiteful Jessie could be with you when she thinks no one else is around."

Veronica found herself smiling.

"And I can tell by the look on your face that I'm several years late with that observation." Cole was restlessly slapping the work gloves he had in one hand into the palm of the other.

"Better late than never," Veronica hazarded as she tugged the soiled garden glove back on her hand. The action drew Cole's gaze downward. He glanced toward the flower bed where she'd been working, and Veronica watched him closely for any sign of disapproval.

She hadn't asked permission to weed the overgrown beds. The bright Sunday morning air had enticed her out and since it was her regular day off, she'd planned to spend the day recovering some of the straggly perennials from the weeds. Cole turned and walked toward the house, wordlessly surveying the garbage bag of weeds and debris she'd gleaned and the extra bag she hadn't opened yet. The dark earth around each little plant she'd saved had been tilled with a hand rake, then carefully watered.

"I hope you don't mind." She spoke to Cole's uncommunicative back. He didn't answer right away. Instead he crouched down and tenderly ran a finger beneath a mum leaf.

"It's a wonder any of these have survived." Cole spoke so softly that Veronica almost thought he was talking to himself. "For quite a while after Jackie died, I had someone keep these up. I guess I haven't thought too much about them lately." Cole was quiet and Veronica sensed he was remembering.

Suddenly the tragedy of Jackie's death and how hard Cole must have taken it brought a wave of sadness over her. It was apparent that Cole had been very much in love with Jackie, and in his letters to Veronica, Hank had always said that if it hadn't been for Curtis, Cole might not have recovered.

How different Cole was from the way she remembered him. And now that she was getting to know him, she found him to be the reverse of the harsh unfriendly stepbrother she could never please as an adolescent.

Her gentle heart suddenly constricted with sadness and compassion, and Veronica felt, to her consternation, the welling of tears in her eyes. Cole stood up, and self-consciously, she tried to blink the tears away before they could fall, but Cole had already seen. He stepped closer.

"I'm such a sentimental sap," she kidded, smiling sheepishly. A warm callus-toughened palm came up to cup her cheek. Her eyes had cleared now and were fixed on the compelling blue of Cole's. Veronica's senses began to reel as Cole's lips came over her in a tender chaste kiss.

In the next moment, his other hand circled her waist and pressed her almost fiercely against the hard thrust of his hips. The tenderness vanished at the burst of raw hunger in his kiss. Her mouth opened, craving more, and Cole needed no clearer invitation. She fairly melted in his arms as his tongue did things to hers that left her trembling, her insides like warm butter.

"I want you, Ronnie," he murmured against her lips. "I think I'd do just about anything to keep you here with me."

Reality whirled away into the distance, and Veronica wondered if she'd just imagined Cole's words. He moved his lips to the soft flesh of her throat, then nibbled a path to her ear.

"Will you stay?" his warm mouth whispered. "It will be good between us, Ronnie."

Veronica's heart thrilled to the velvet edge of his gruff voice, to the sensual promise of more of this taste of heaven. At first she resisted the weak intrusion of sanity, as her slumberous eyes opened to the passion-blackened depths of his.

"What I feel for you just won't go away," he was saying. Veronica was too lovestruck to recognize the difference between what she'd longed to hear from Cole and what he'd actually said. Joy welled up inside and Veronica pulled his mouth back to hers, taking her turn at loving aggression. Cole's ragged breathing mingled with hers, his arms tightening almost painfully around her slenderness. Now she recognized the difference between the love she'd thought she'd felt for Eric and the blinding intensity of the love she now had for Cole.

"If we don't stop this..." he murmured. "Just stand still for a moment." Veronica was only too happy to comply, delighted that Cole was struggling to restrain his arousal—his arousal for her. He released her slowly.

"Curtis will think I've forgotten about him." Cole's lips quirked before they came down on hers for a last brief kiss. Then he was leaning down for her fallen crutches. "We'll take up where we left off after Curtis goes to bed tonight," he promised in a rough whisper.

Veronica was helpless to keep her eyes from following Cole as he started to walk away from her toward the back of the house. He turned momentarily, his eyes still burning as they raked over her in a promise of possession that sent a fresh flood of weakness through her system. Then he disappeared around the corner of the house and went inside.

SANITY DIDN'T RETURN IMMEDIATELY, and Veronica had finished her work in the flowerbed before niggling little doubts began to creep in. Facing Cole over the kitchen table at lunch with a sullen little Curtis between them had brought what was really happening into clearer focus. By supper that evening, Veronica's feet had finally touched earth.

I want you, Ronnie...it will be good between us...I'm afraid I won't be able to wait... again and again Cole's words paraded through her mind. *We'll take up where we left off after Curtis goes to bed tonight,* he had said.

Cole was offering her an affair.

Veronica squeezed her eyes closed and felt like an idiot. How had she let her love for Cole get so out of hand that she'd been unable to understand what he had so clearly said? If she'd doubted her sanity after Eric deserted her, she was certain she was more than a little crazy now. And when Cole came to her room as he seemed to have every intention of doing, how would he react when he saw her scars and found out the truth about her marriage to Eric?

Heartsick, Veronica realized she had to seek him out—talk to him, make some excuse. Perhaps she could defuse the whole situation before it blew up in her face.

Veronica moved nervously into the hall, then stopped. She was as close now as she was going to come to telling Cole everything about her marriage to Eric. *Would that be so bad,* she asked herself.

Before she'd come back to Wyoming, she'd dreaded Cole's finding out about her marriage to Eric because of her fear that he'd either make the obvious comparison between her and her mother, or worse, tell her outright he wasn't surprised that Eric had wised up and dumped her before he'd consummated the marriage. Getting to know Cole better had slowly eroded those fears, but what would Cole say if she admitted her lack of experience and told him she wouldn't, couldn't, let their relationship go any further? Forcing herself to get it over with, Veronica moved down the hall to the den.

Cole looked up when she stepped into the doorway. Seeing her, he leaned back in the big chair behind his desk, his gaze lazily appraising her slender body. For the umpteenth time that day, Veronica was reminded of the ugliness he'd see if he saw her unclothed.

Funny how she'd consoled herself with the psychologist's assurances that the man who truly fell in love with her would not mind the scars. Now that she'd come this close to intimacy with Cole, she realized she hadn't really believed those assurances.

"I'd like to talk to you, Cole." Veronica suddenly had trouble maintaining eye contact with the roving gaze that had returned to rest on her flushed face.

"I was just finishing up in here," Cole said, his look gently chiding her for what he must have assumed was impatience.

"What we need to talk about has to be discussed before then," she said, her voice as firm and as determined as she could manage.

"Having second thoughts?" There was only a touch of sternness in Cole's voice. From the almost indulgent smile on his face Veronica knew he was confident that a few kisses would remove any reservations she might have acquired since late morning. It also confirmed that Cole did indeed intend for them to make love.

Veronica was extremely apprehensive and her hands clenched and unclenched on the crutch grips. "I misled you this morning, Cole," she began, watching the slight narrowing of his eyes. "Not intentionally," she hurried to add, "but I just got...carried away. I know it was unfair of me to allow you to think I would be willing to..." She paused nervously. "I guess I wasn't...thinking clearly." Her stumbling speech must have sounded absurd. "I'm sorry."

Cole's expression turned flintlike before he glanced away from her, a crease forming slowly between his dark brows. When his eyes came back to hers, she could discern nothing of what he was thinking other than he must be angry with her.

"Do you want something a little more permanent than what you thought I was offering this morning?" Cole's gaze was intent, and probing.

"I don't want you to misunderstand me," she said, her voice sounding abysmally virginal. "I realize you can't offer me a permanent relationship—not that I'm trying to pressure or coerce you into one," she assured him hastily, her mouth going dry. "But I can't have an affair with you." Cole stared at her steadily, unnerving her with his ongoing silence.

"Do you want some kind of commitment from me?" A speculative gleam darkened his eyes.

"I'm not asking for one, Cole."

"But there can be nothing more between us if I don't make one," he surmised grimly, yet without anger.

"That's right," Veronica murmured, suddenly unable to think of anything but the promise of heaven she was forcing herself to give up.

"Then I guess I'll see you at breakfast." Cole's total attention returned to what he'd been working on when she'd interrupted. Veronica accepted the aloof dismissal and retreated dismally to her room.

CHAPTER NINE

FOR THE NEXT TWO WEEKS, Veronica's life settled into a pattern of work and exercise. She walked a mile a day and took Honey Lamb out regularly, riding the gentle mare around a small pasture near one of the barns where the gregarious Shorty was within shouting distance.

The increase in exercise had been hard on her, but in the past day or so her body seemed to have adjusted and her physical therapist was pleased with her progress. She would be trading in her crutches for a walking cane any time now and she was eager for the change.

She saw Cole only at mealtimes, unless he was in the house doing paperwork. Even then, if she wasn't preparing a meal or cleaning up after one, she slipped outside for a walk or to work in the flower beds.

Curtis was home a lot more, but he was with Cole, except when Cole went out for the evening. Then Shorty or Teddy's teenaged sister, Brenda, would come in.

Veronica had a lot of early nights, partly because she was worn out by seven-thirty, but more because she didn't want to know when Cole came home. She'd heard enough speculation from Shorty to guess that on most evenings Cole was with Jessie.

It hurt that Cole could so quickly and completely turn to pursuing Jessie. But it was just as well, she told herself, that she'd seen how easily the shallow interest Cole had shown in her could be switched to someone else. If Veronica had entertained any fairy-tale notions about Cole being the man of her dreams, they were gone now.

Cole's remoteness made Veronica feel they were no longer even friends. She could see that soon she would find living in the same house with Cole and his recalcitrant son intolerable.

"YOUR MOTHER CALLED while you were in town," Cole said as he came into the kitchen for a glass of iced tea. Veronica had just returned from a session with the physical therapist and was tiredly contemplating a nap before she started dinner preparations.

"I'll call her later," Veronica replied as she tossed her car keys onto their usual spot beside the sugar canister.

"She sounded upset," Cole added, and Veronica allowed herself to look at Cole for the first time since he'd come into the room.

Unfair! her heart cried when she was suddenly weakened by the sight of Cole leaning against the counter, sipping his tea, his indolent pose reminding Veronica what it felt like to be pressed against the length of his solidly male form. Unaware that Cole had seen both the slow sweep of her violet eyes and the tinge of color that had come into her cheeks, Veronica tried to bring her attention back to what he had just said.

"What did she want?" Veronica was too tired to waste any of her available rest time on the phone for a false alarm. Sometimes her mother tended to exaggerate.

"She was upset with me," Cole said, the quirk of his lips telling her what he thought of that.

"It seems to me we agreed you would be polite to my mother," she reminded him, a touch of anger coming into eyes that had seemed almost spiritless to Cole for the past two weeks.

"I was the perfect gentleman," he assured her. "Even when she jumped all over me for taking advantage of you."

A frown crossed Veronica's face. "Where did she get an idea like that?" She could think of nothing she'd said that would have given her mother that impression.

"She doesn't like the idea of your working for me. She says I've taken advantage of your generosity long enough."

"Mother said that?" Veronica couldn't imagine her mother standing up to Cole or challenging him in any way. Men like Cole had always cowed her.

"That, and more." Cole sipped his drink, watching her over the top of the glass.

"More?"

"She's afraid you're going to fall in love with me." High color stung her cheeks at Cole's words. "She's afraid you're too vulnerable after what Eric did to you."

Veronica was mortified. What else had her mother told him?

"I apologize. I'm sorry Mother jumped to such awkward conclusions." Veronica hastened across the room toward the phone extension. "I guess this is one call that shouldn't wait." Veronica hoped her brisk manner would assure Cole that her mother's fears were unfounded. She couldn't let either of them know that it was a little late for motherly concern.

She had just begun to dial the number when Cole came up behind her and slipped his arms around her waist. Enveloped in the electric warmth that pressed against the entire length of her body, Veronica misdialed. Surprise brought her head around just in time for her lips to brush

Cole's. But before she could succumb to their firm sensuality she turned her face away again, then silently endured a further shock to her system when Cole nudged aside her shoulder-length hair and began placing slow lingering kisses on her neck just beneath her ear.

Lethargy spread through her system, clouding rational thought. She opened her mouth to voice some false words of vague outrage and heard herself give a melting sigh. Cole evidently took that for encouragement and nuzzled against her ear before he traced the delicate shell with his tongue and nibbled the sensitive lobe.

"Now," Cole whispered with husky satisfaction when he felt her go slack in his arms. "Now you can tell your mother all about how living with me hasn't affected you much one way or the other."

It took a few seconds for Cole's gently mocking words to penetrate the seductive haze. When they did, Veronica made a movement of protest and Cole released her to accommodate her step away from him.

She had just turned toward him, her face awash in embarrassed color, when he picked up his glass of iced tea and left the kitchen. Veronica put down the telephone receiver, then picked it up again and shakily redialed, hoping her mother would not detect the tremor in her voice or the confusion in her less-than-honest denials.

"ARE YOU CERTAIN this is what you want to do?" Helen's voice, coming from the hall outside Cole's bedroom, reached Veronica's ears.

Her fitful nap was due to be over soon, but the sounds of activity in the house awakened her a few minutes earlier than she had planned. She stepped into the bathroom and ran a brush through her hair hoping to give

Helen a chance to go back into the main part of the house. Evidently she had arrived with Curtis.

But when Veronica went out into the hall, she heard Helen in Cole's bedroom. As she reached the doorway, she could see Helen and Cole standing in front of the large closet, boxes littering the floor nearby. Cole happened to glance Veronica's way and she allowed his gaze to hold hers only momentarily before she continued past the door on her way to the kitchen.

"Hello, Curtis," Veronica called cheerfully as she entered the kitchen. Curtis mumbled a response but didn't favor her with a look. Standing on the counter top in his dusty sneakers, he was busy going through one of the upper cupboards.

"What are you looking for?" Veronica hoped to find some way of getting his dirty shoes off the counter without directly asking the boy to get down.

"I'm hungry," Curtis announced.

"There's some fruit in the refrigerator, but if you'd rather have something else, the cookie jar is full. Just be sure you put the milk away if you get it out." Veronica made her way to the sink and washed her hands while she waited for Curtis to get down. But when she turned around again, he was digging into another shelf.

"Why don't you get down from the counter, Curtis? There's nothing up there but canned goods and baking supplies."

"No."

"Come on, Curtis," Veronica prompted, pasting a neutral smile on her face as she crossed to the boy and touched his arm. Curtis jerked away as if her fingers had burned him, but Veronica gave every impression of not noticing. "You get out the milk and I'll put some cookies on a plate."

Her suggestion was ignored. Curtis continued to shove canned goods around, making chaos of the precise placement Veronica made in order to keep better track of what to buy on her weekly grocery trips to town. She and Cole had spent a lot of time organizing what Curtis was so pointlessly disrupting.

"Can you read the labels on those cans?" she asked as he moved to a lower shelf and continued to rummage.

"I can read," he answered sulkily, and Veronica felt her irritation rising at the boy's continual show of defiance.

"Good," she said. "Then when you've finished looking for something that's not up there, you can go back and put every can and box back exactly the way you found it." That earned her Curtis's complete, although hostile, attention.

"That's your job." Those words had become Curtis's pet refrain.

"Normally it is," Veronica agreed, her patient-sounding voice and manner worthy of an award. "But when you come along and make a mess of my work, I think it's only fair that you fix it. It's a good way to make certain you don't make the same mistake again."

"This is my house—mine and my dad's," Curtis corrected. "You just work here." Curtis returned to what he was doing, obviously satisfied that the matter had been dealt with.

"I hope you aren't this rude to everyone, Curtis," Veronica commented before she braced herself for more unpleasantness. "You can begin with the top shelf."

There was complete silence for a fraction of a second before Curtis gave the canned goods on the lower shelf a parting shove. The cupboard door banged shut and

Curtis started to get down. Veronica stepped deliberately into his path.

"I don't have to do what you want." Curtis's sassy look was far removed from the solemn-eyed reserve she'd once found so adorable.

She was suddenly reminded of how she'd felt when a new man began making inroads into her mother's life. After Jessie's comment that day two weeks ago, Curtis likely believed her presence threatened Jessie's relationship with his father. Despite her momentary irritation with the boy, Veronica felt compassion for him, concerned about the needless worry he was being put through. Nevertheless she didn't intend to allow Curtis to bully her.

"I'm afraid you do this time, Curtis," she said firmly. "I need to start working on your supper." They stared at each other for a moment, defiance sparkling in his gray eyes before they wavered toward a movement in the doorway to the hall. Instantly his little lip thrust out endearingly and his gray eyes went tragically woebegone.

"What's going on, Veronica?" Helen demanded as she bustled across the room and reached to cuddle Curtis protectively in her arms.

"Curtis just made a shambles of this cupboard and I told him he had to straighten it up," Veronica told her.

"Oh, for heaven's sake!" Helen scolded as she pulled Curtis down from the cupboard, forcing Veronica to move aside quickly or collide with the boy's body. "This kitchen is your responsibility, not Curtis's." Helen gave Curtis a nudge toward the porch door. "Go on outside and play until supper." Curtis hurried out, his face the picture of childish glee.

Veronica was trembling with anger. "Please don't ever interfere like that again," she told Helen once Curtis was safely out of earshot. "I'm having enough problems with him without you rushing in to take his side and cast me in the role of villain."

"Someone needed to take the boy's side just now and I intend to speak to Cole about what just happened," Helen said huffily.

"Go ahead," Veronica invited, keeping her voice even. "But be sure to tell him all of it. Cole can come in and see for himself what has become of the cupboards we spent all that time organizing."

Helen looked a bit disconcerted at that, but Veronica didn't give her a chance to say more. She moved aside to another section of cupboards and noisily began taking out the things she needed to start supper. Wordlessly Helen left, easing the angry tension in the room.

"WHAT'S COLE DOIN'?" Shorty asked as he started laying out the Scrabble game he was so fond of playing. "I seen all them boxes he hauled outta here and put in Helen's car." Veronica smiled at Shorty's avid hunger for gossip. It was something he didn't even pretend to suppress.

"I think they were Jackie's things, but he didn't say," she replied as she set the controls on the dishwasher and started it.

"You didn't ask?" Shorty would have, but Veronica was not quite so bold, especially since she was almost certain she was right. Cole would probably not appreciate any questions from her about Jackie. Veronica shook her head and Shorty grunted.

"I noticed Curtis's got his ma's picture on his lamp table. It was the one that was in Cole's den from the looks of the frame." Shorty's voice lowered. "Once I seen that,

I noticed Jackie's wedding keepsakes were gone out of the china cabinet in the dining room.''

"Shorty!" Veronica scolded. "You are without a doubt the most..." She hesitated, a teasing grin on her face. "Let's just say you're observant."

"Observant?" Shorty looked somewhat offended.

"I'm too polite to tell you I think you're nosy. Observant sounded much more tactful," Veronica said, then giggled when Shorty pointed at her waggishly.

"You'd better watch that, gal," he threatened. "T-a-c-t don't get as many points in Scrabble as n-o-s-y does," he said, referring to the point values the game gave each letter.

"Is that so?" Veronica challenged as she stationed herself across the table from the weathered old cowhand. "You're going to have to think of some more clever uses for any high-value letters you happen to draw tonight," she warned him playfully. "I plan to give you a little stronger competition than I did last time."

Veronica was a bit embarrassed to admit it, but when she and Shorty first started playing Scrabble together, she hadn't expected him to be so good at a vocabulary game. Her rather low expectations had left her unprepared for her repeated losses to him. Shorty might have been one of the most casual speakers she'd ever known, but his reading vocabulary was really quite vast.

"It looks to me like the boss is fixin' to pop the question on someone about any time now," Shorty piped up later as he carefully laid out the right combination of letters on high-value spaces to earn himself twenty-seven points. Veronica added the total to Shorty's rapidly climbing score, his statement bringing a pain she could barely conceal from her pale features.

"Do you think he's really ready to remarry?" she managed in her best casual manner, shocked at the realization that she found the thought of Cole's remarrying intolerable.

"Yep, I do."

Veronica laid out the letters for her next word and silently counted up the pitifully low number of points it gained her. Suddenly she just wanted to finish the game—anything to hasten the end of this distressing turn of conversation.

"Course, at this point, it's mighty hard to tell which one the boss'll choose," Shorty jabbered on.

"What do you mean, which one?" Veronica couldn't help asking. Was there someone besides Jessie? "I thought you said Cole was seeing Jessie nearly every evening."

"I didn't say that," Shorty corrected as he rearranged the letters on his rack. "He mighta gone over to see her once or twice, but he had some business with her daddy. Besides, I got my own private thoughts as to where he's been takin' hisself off to."

With that, Shorty fell maddeningly silent and Veronica tried to focus on the game. She chanced a look up every now and then, as if she could tell from Shorty's weathered face what thoughts he was keeping to himself. But all she could detect was the same unwavering concentration that would likely make tonight's game another one of his triumphs.

Veronica rested her chin on her hand and continued to stare unseeingly at the letters she'd drawn. Her thoughts moved back into the same track they'd followed for hours, trying to find the logic in Cole's sensual assault that afternoon.

The only conclusion that made any sense was that he'd been irritated by her mother's call and had taken some kind of perverse pleasure in making certain Veronica would have a problem convincing her mother she had been unaffected by him. In her romantic heart of hearts, she hoped he'd done it because he really did feel something for her and didn't want her to deny there was nothing between them. But, Veronica reminded herself, those kind of romantic fairy-tales happened only to others.

"There's a lot of that goin' around," Shorty said. Veronica had only half heard Shorty's comment.

"Hmm?"

Shorty pointed to the word he'd just laid out.

"D-a-y-d-r-e-a-m," Shorty spelled aloud, then chuckled. "Seems to be affectin' two-thirds of the people who live in this house."

Veronica's gaze turned away from the teasing in Shorty's dark eyes as a heavy blush settled on her cheeks. She quickly tallied the score he'd managed to get by adding the word "dream" to the "day" she'd put down. The fact that the "m" covered the triple-word space set his score even further ahead of hers.

The little lackluster word Veronica put down next failed to get her any substantial point count, but it forced Shorty to return to contemplating the five letters he'd just drawn and kept him from making any more observations about her and Cole. At least she assumed Shorty had meant her and Cole. He certainly hadn't been talking about Curtis.

Veronica's attention was drawn to the sound of Cole's pickup coming up the driveway. She'd hoped to finish this game long before Cole returned, and now she fidgeted impatiently with her letter tiles while she waited for Shorty to play.

Cole's booted feet clunked up the porch steps and into the kitchen almost before she could adjust to his unexpected return. The black Stetson made its usual twirling arc toward the coat tree in the corner and managed to catch the same hook it always did. A wide grin split the usual sternness of Cole's demeanor as his eyes flicked from Shorty and lingered warmly on Veronica.

"Is Curtis in bed?" he asked as he turned a kitchen chair backward and sat astride it, his thickly muscled forearms resting on the chair back as he watched the game that was clearly in its last moments.

"Yep." Shorty was too intent on the letters in his rack to say more.

Veronica was trying to summon at least a pretense of interest in the game she'd already lost, but the steady look Cole was giving her made it hard to concentrate. Poor Shorty. Her preoccupation hadn't made the game much of a challenge for him.

"How did that talk with your mother go, Ronnie?"

Fresh color flooded Veronica's cheeks. She glanced in Cole's direction and encountered the same knowing glimmer in his eyes that had mocked her response to him that afternoon.

"Just as you planned it to," she answered, a trace of irritation in her soft reply as she pointlessly rearranged the letters in her rack.

Shorty chuckled as he laid out his remaining letters, again using a word she'd just put on the board to add another thirty points to his score. And just when Veronica thought the old cowhand had been concentrating too hard on the game to pay attention to the veiled conversation between her and Cole, she saw him give them both a sly wink.

Veronica couldn't see any way to use her last three letters to tie Shorty's score, much less win the game. Besides, now that Cole was home, she was especially eager to end the game.

"You win again," she conceded good-naturedly, then helped Shorty clear the board and put the game away. Shorty stood up, stretched, then walked to the coat tree for his hat before he turned back toward Veronica.

"Don't forget," he cautioned, pointing at her just as she was rising from her chair. "Playin' at Scrabble is a lot like what some say about playin' at cards."

Veronica was focused so intently on escaping Cole's presence that Shorty's words didn't make much sense at first.

"What?"

"You think on it," he advised with a wink. "It'll come to you in a second." With that, the old man was out the porch door, whistling a merry tune.

"What he means is 'Lucky at cards, unlucky in love,'" Cole recounted, then chuckled. Veronica's gaze continued to shy from his.

"I don't put a lot of faith in an old saw," she told him as she grasped her crutches and turned to leave the kitchen.

"What about the one, 'The way to a man's heart is through his stomach'?" Cole rose from his chair and turned it around to slide it under the table. Veronica forced a laugh to cover her inner reaction to that particular saying.

"If that was true, Mrs. Engstrom would still be here, colorful dialect and all," she joked, then started for her room as Cole crossed the stretch of floor between them. "Good night."

Cole caught her arm, stopping her before she could take another step.

"I'm tired, Cole," she said quickly, frightened by the wave of sensation that rocked her slim frame and sent a burst of heat into the deepest part of her. Veronica was unaware of the hunted look in the violet depths of her eyes, which had flown to his, unable to avoid their determined cobalt glints. They stood staring at each other for a long moment before Cole stepped close and lifted her chin with the side of a lean finger.

"Don't," she whispered as his lips lowered to hers. Cole allowed her to turn her face away slightly, but the light touch of his finger slid upward to trace a pattern of sensation on her flushed cheek.

"Would it help to apologize for the other night?" he asked huskily as the fingers of his other hand slid along the line of her jaw and combed gently into her hair.

"An apology won't change anything," she said, her eyes sparkling with resentment when they shot back to his—resentment that he thought an apology would get her into bed with him!

"Oh, but it will," he rasped confidently, his voice going softer.

"But I wo—"

Cole's finger tapped silencingly on her lips. "I don't expect you to," he assured her, smiling gently. "Friends again?" His dark brows arched and Veronica felt herself unfairly swayed by what she must have been mistaking for anxiety in his eyes.

"All right," she said at last.

Cole's mouth settled tenderly on hers before he drew away, his lips stretched in a satisfied smile.

"Then good night, Ronnie," he whispered.

Veronica stared up into his eyes for a confused moment before she turned and headed to her room.

CHAPTER TEN

COLE WAS IMMEDIATELY AWARE that something had happened the moment Veronica entered the den.

Her cheeks were burning with anger and humiliation, and her eyes held glimmers of hurt. The way she tossed the set of keys onto the desk in front of him betrayed more than average irritation, and Cole rose swiftly to his feet.

"What is it, Ronnie?" he demanded gently.

"You'll have to go pick up Curtis from Helen's yourself," she said, and he sensed rather than saw that she was about to burst into tears.

"Why? What's wrong?"

Her battle to control her hurt and anger was nearly lost when she tried to explain. The memory of Curtis's frightened gray eyes cut into her heart afresh. She had no explanation for the boy's sudden inexplicable fear of her and it hurt unbearably to think of it, much less tell Cole.

"Curtis didn't want to get into the car with me," she managed, her voice wavering. Cole came around the desk, his iron visage mildly alarming. "Curtis—" Veronica took a deep breath to steady herself "—Curtis was frightened of me and..." Veronica's throat closed up in a spasm of hurt.

"And what?" Cole caught her upper arms gently and bent slightly to look closely into her tear-stung eyes.

What could Veronica tell him? Helen was Jackie's sister. How could she tell him about the humiliating way Helen had taken Curtis aside and hugged him protectively while she coldly ordered Veronica off her front porch? Helen had seemed glad of both Curtis's reluctance to go with her and the opportunity to send Veronica home to Cole without his son.

"Helen didn't think it was a good idea to send Curtis home with me," she told him, struggling to remind herself that Helen had been sensible not to send the boy with someone he mistrusted.

"The hell you say!" Cole burst out. Veronica tried to shrink out of his grip, and instantly his harshness softened. "I'm not angry with you, Ronnie," he assured her, but when he started to pull her into his arms, she put up a firm hand to deny herself the comfort of his broad chest.

How it had hurt to see another display of Curtis's inability to tolerate her! And now something had made him mistrustful—and worse—frightened of her. But what?

"Let's go get this straightened out." Cole hadn't commented on Veronica's sudden resistance to his nearness, but when he sensed she was doing so to withdraw from him emotionally, he pulled her closer. "Whatever this is between you and Curtis is going to change," he promised. "I'll see to it."

Veronica shook her head. "You can't force the boy to like me, Cole. Besides," she reasoned, "it's not as if I'm going to be living here indefinitely. Let's just leave him alone." Cole's grip on her arms tightened.

"I won't have my son behave this way without provocation," he said gruffly.

"How do you know I haven't done something to cause all this?" she challenged. Cole's gaze never wavered.

"Because I know you," he said quietly.

Veronica was instantly angry.

"Because you think you know me," she corrected. "What do you really know about me?" Her demand hung heavily between them. "I could tell you a few stories about men my mother thought she knew. I used to cause a lot of problems for her with each new suitor, but at least when I was frightened of one, she'd give credence to what I told her. How can you do less?"

Cole's mouth tightened grimly. "The fact that you're taking the boy's side against yourself only reinforces my trust in you, Ronnie," he told her stubbornly. "But I intend to get to the bottom of this." Cole's somber countenance was intimidating. "Let's go." He had started to guide her to the door when she pulled back.

"This should just be between you and your family. My presence might color any explanations you get." Veronica was barely aware of the way her hands were twisting on the crutch grips.

Cole seemed to accept her refusal, but before he turned to go and pick up Curtis from Helen's, he bent to place a quick kiss on the unrelaxed line of her lips, leaving a warmth that lingered long after he turned away. Veronica listened to his booted stride continue through the silent house until the porch door closed. It was then that the brimming wetness in her eyes coursed disconsolately down her cheeks.

COLE SIGHED HEAVILY as he leaned back in the porch swing where Veronica had spent a good share of the evening alone.

"He won't talk to me." Cole's deep voice was husky with frustration as he automatically set the wide swing in motion with the rhythmic bunch and release of his powerful thigh muscles. Veronica relaxed and allowed Cole's easy strength to rock her as she inhaled the warm night air and caught a whiff of the masculine scent of soap and after-shave she associated exclusively with Cole.

"Where is he now?" It distressed her that her presence had divided father and son.

"He's confined to his room for the rest of the evening." Cole's irritable tone betrayed his hurt. He was just as bewildered as she by Curtis's behavior.

"Please don't be impatient with him," she urged. "And don't treat him harshly. He'll not only blame me, but your relationship with him is too precious to risk for the sake of an outsider."

Cole cursed roundly and turned toward her in the swing, his abrupt movement destroying the rhythm and bringing the swing to a lurching halt.

"You're no outsider," he growled as he pulled her roughly to himself. "You're—" The grooves on each side of his well-carved mouth deepened in exasperation when he couldn't seem to finish the sentence. Veronica was pressing against his chest trying to separate them before the raw sensuality she sensed in Cole was released. But it was too late.

Cole's lips captured hers as he crushed her to him. All thoughts of resistance vanished beneath the insistent pressure of the hard mouth that mastered hers and drew her into the emotional whirlwind that claimed them both. She had no thought of refusal when Cole's hand came between them to unfasten a few buttons of her blouse before his vanquishing lips wandered lower.

Fierce, possessive, drugging. Cole's mouth set every nerve ending writhing in sensuous torture as he kissed a trail to the shadowy cleavage of her breasts. Veronica was breathless when she felt the front of her bra being unclasped. Then a sharp intrusion of fear suddenly had her clutching at her blouse, struggling to cover herself. But the lean fingers that restrained hers were stronger.

"Please don't." The anguish in her voice stopped him. Cole placed a couple of coaxing kisses on each corner of her love-swollen lips, but at last her resistance made him stop.

"What's wrong?"

Veronica felt her reserve weaken at the tenderness in Cole's voice. He wasn't angry, only perplexed. One look at the concern in the darkened depths of his eyes was almost too persuasive for her to resist.

"I'm...I'm..." Veronica paused, licking her dry lips. "There was a lot of twisted metal in the accident." Her voice wavered hoping Cole would take the hint without her having to explain further, but he didn't seem to understand. "I've got a lot of ugly scars," she whispered, her gaze dropping to his collar. She couldn't bear to watch the revulsion that would surely come next.

The large hand that had caught her small frantic ones pulled her slim fingers away from the front of her blouse. Panicked eyes shot back to his face. In spite of what she'd just told him, she read the determination on his iron features and went still in his arms. Her dark-lashed lids drifted closed at the tender intrusion of his fingers into the V of her clothing, then crept open, unable to keep her eyes from his face. A part of her sensed Cole would not react in a hurtful way, and that sudden bit of intuition enabled her to endure the next few seconds.

Cole released her hands. Slowly he parted the front facings of her blouse, then gently pushed away the concealing lace of one side of her bra. Veronica trembled as her unscarred breast was bared to his gaze. Tides of em-

barrassed color came into her face as Cole's breath
started coming unsteadily.

Without prolonging her discomfort more than necessary, Cole uncovered her other breast. Blue eyes that
missed nothing followed the still-vivid scarring along her
shoulder that dwindled to a jagged red seam that slashed
over the outer curve of her right breast to just below the
nipple. The natural symmetry of the silken mound had
been altered only slightly. Cole gently traced his thumb
over the breast section of the scar before he abruptly
lowered his dark head.

"No!"

The strong fingers that had just touched her breast in-
tercepted the hand she put up to keep him away, his firm
grip making resistance impossible. Veronica gasped in
pleasure as his teeth closed tenderly around the dusky tip,
his tongue teasing the nipple to full hardness. Veronica
had to bite her lip to keep from crying out. All her fear
vanished in the flash fire of sensation Cole kindled in her.
Her hand was released and Veronica clutched at his
shoulders, her head slowly dropping back in sensual surrender as his mouth journeyed to her other breast for a
few bone-melting moments. By the time his mouth made
an unhurried ascent to her lips she was liquid in his arms.

"Sometimes it amazes me how worked up women get
about such damned trivial things as scars," he growled
against her mouth, then took her lower lip between his
teeth and gave it a reproving tug. "There are other qualities more important to me than physical perfection,
Veronica, and I think it's about time you realized it."

The stern angles of Cole's face had softened, and the
deep blue of his eyes revealed tender sincerity. Veronica
felt soul-liberating relief. Cole hadn't found her repulsive. His unexpected acceptance of her body restored

much of the self-esteem she'd struggled for months to regain.

For the first time since the accident Veronica realized that the consequences of that tragic ride were not quite as final as she'd first believed. It was gradually dawning on her that she really would recover fully, that her life could be salvaged, her personal goals resurrected.

Cole brought his hands around to her blouse front, one corner of his mouth curved in self-directed mockery. "There's nothing like getting carried away on a porch swing with the audience potential this one has," he said as he nodded toward the barn and outbuildings that included the bunkhouse. Capable fingers fastened her bra and slowly rebuttoned her blouse. Then he was kissing her again and the tremor that went through her echoed in Cole's large frame.

"This has to stop," he rasped between kisses, but he was pulling her even harder against himself, making the extent of his arousal clear. Reluctantly Veronica summoned what was left of her modesty, striving to remind herself that any of Cole's men could look toward the house and see them.

Veronica pulled her arms from around his neck and slipped her hands between herself and Cole. He accepted the wordless signal, but Veronica sensed the effort it cost him to relax. Even when she decided he had there was a tenseness about him that indicated he could easily become aroused again.

"Do you mind if I ask what Helen had to say about this afternoon?" she ventured, hoping her question would distract them both. Cole loosened his embrace. "Has she had any insight at all into what caused Curtis to be frightened of me?"

Cole shifted on the swing, then stretched his long legs out in front of him. Keeping her against his side, his arm resting more casually around her shoulders, Cole sighed and set the swing in motion again.

"Helen can't figure it out, either," he said, "but she insisted she was right not to send Curtis with you." The frustration had come back into his voice, and Veronica again regretted that her presence was causing problems.

"I think she was right, too." Veronica meant what she said, no matter how angry Helen had made her or how hurt she'd been at Curtis's refusal. However, she wasn't ready to believe that Helen didn't know why Curtis was frightened of her. Other than Cole, Helen was the one person who spent hours at a time with the boy. It didn't take much to conclude that Helen's disapproval and dislike of her had been picked up by Curtis. Veronica tried not to think about the possibility that the boy had actually been encouraged not to like her.

"I didn't come out here to talk about Helen," Cole said gruffly, as his gaze turned from staring into the distance to find her face in the slowly dwindling light. "I've started making plans for a camping trip this weekend." Cole's voice had lowered, implying that his plan included her.

Deliberately misunderstanding, Veronica smiled and said, "That sounds like fun, Cole. Curtis will love having you to himself for an entire weekend. Maybe a couple of days together will make up for the problems my being here has caused you both." Her eyes shied away from the instant exasperation on Cole's face.

"But you're the most important part of my plan, Ronnie," he said. "Did you ever learn to fish?" Cole gave her a reassuring squeeze.

"This isn't a good idea," Veronica insisted, shaking her head. She had to look away from the glimmer of purpose in Cole's eyes as she searched for some way to discourage him. "I can't go, Cole. What about the sleeping arrangements? What will Curtis think about the three of us going off to the woods together?"

"I've thought of all that. You'll have your own tent and Curtis and I will bunk together in the bigger one. Besides, this will give you two an opportunity to spend some time together away from the ranch. I want him to get used to us being together."

Veronica tried not to think about Cole's last remark and her excuses continued. Cole merely smiled at her hasty attempts to dissuade him, patiently listening to every point she made before firmly rejecting each one. His mind was made up. Nothing would disrupt his weekend plans for three.

"TIRED?" Cole grinned down at Veronica as he pulled up the tent stake she'd just started to pound into the ground. She watched as he stretched the tent rope and repositioned the stake several inches beyond where she had struggled to place it. With a wry twist to her lips, she followed on her hands and knees.

"Here's the hammer," Veronica said, offering it to Cole, but he shook his head, his hand gripping the tent stake.

"Go ahead. I trust you."

Veronica raised the mallet, then glanced up at his smiling face. "Are you sure?"

"The longer you hesitate, the less sure I get. If you miss and smash my hand instead, at least it's the last stake." His smile widened to a grin.

Veronica grinned back, then fixed her eyes on the head of the stake and carefully pounded it into the ground. When she finished, Cole took the hammer and helped her to her feet.

"Come on, Curtis," Cole yelled toward the truck. "Let's get that gear over here." While she and Cole were putting up the tents, Curtis was supposed to be unloading the truck so they could set up their campsite. But so far he'd managed only a few things and these he'd placed near the ring of smoke-blackened rocks left by a previous camper.

Veronica glanced around the campsite, which stood in a small clearing surrounded by dense forest, and took a savoring breath of the clean pine-scented air. So far, the day had been ideal. After a quick breakfast at the ranch, Cole had loaded the truck and they had set off for the Laramie Mountains, leaving Shorty and the other men to fend for themselves for the weekend. Cole had offered to share cooking duties with Veronica on the trip, and since Curtis had been a model of good behavior, Veronica was beginning to feel more optimistic about their two days and one night together.

Cole went over to hurry Curtis along and Veronica unzipped the flaps of the tents, which were set up side by side, to begin tossing their bedrolls and extra blankets inside. The last things she threw in were the small duffle bags that held their clothing. By the time she'd finished, Cole had deposited the canvas bag of towels and cooking utensils on the small wooden table he'd carried from the truck. Once the campsite was put in order, Cole got out the fishing poles and tackle. Curtis held a Styrofoam cup of worms they'd purchased on the way, avidly interested in the live lures that squirmed in the dirt.

"Let's go get supper." Cole led the way down the slow incline to the small lake, which wasn't visible from their campsite. Veronica followed, carefully using her crutches to negotiate the rocky dirt path that curved haphazardly to the lakeside. Tree roots ribbed the path in spots, making an occasional natural step that leveled out the path slightly before it started downward again. Veronica made her way down with much more ease than she anticipated for the return trip, but she was ecstatic.

Although she'd spent a lot of summers at camp, she never fished, preferring to spend her time swimming or horseback riding. Hank used to promise to take her one day, but he'd never found the time. And as Veronica grew older, she didn't think much about it, adapting to the more ladylike pastimes of her friends.

"How are you doing?" Cole asked as she reached the bank and watched him search through his tackle box for hooks. Curtis was already threading his onto the end of his line like a pro, his young face intent on his work.

"Just great," she returned as Cole unfolded his lean length from a crouch. Veronica paid close attention as he put hooks on her line and his, then gave each pole a quick check. The plaid shirt he wore stretched appealingly over his broad chest and back, emphasizing the effortless play of hard muscle, she noticed, while the comfortably faded jeans he had on clung to his every move, reminding her how it felt to be pressed against the unyielding contours of that length.

"May I try?"

Cole had started to bait her hook when her question stopped him. He grinned, his look telling her he expected her to change her mind. Curtis was suddenly right beside her, holding his Styrofoam cup of bait practically under her nose, his face a picture of glee.

Without missing a beat, Veronica dug into the pungent, earthy-smelling container and pulled out a long fat worm. As she held it at eye level, she glanced down at the small face that was watching for her to make some delicate expression of revulsion. Instead, Veronica smiled.

"I have a recipe somewhere for earthworm cookies. I've always wondered what they'd taste like." Veronica pretended to give the worm a considering look.

"Yuk!" Curtis's face was screwing up disdainfully as Cole started chuckling. Curtis realized then that Veronica was joking and his disdain turned to a childish giggle, then to impish delight. "Hey, how about making some of those cookies for Shorty?"

"What?" Curtis's question caught her off guard, but she suppressed a smile at the boy's uninhibited sense of mischief.

"Shorty is always talking about the weird things his mother made him eat when he was a kid," Curtis explained. "We can see if he recognizes the taste." Curtis was turning the Styrofoam cup this way and that as if counting the number of worms they had left.

"Let's just feed the worms to the fish and forget about earthworm cookies," Cole suggested to his son with mock sternness as he exchanged a sparkling look with Veronica. "Why don't you go ahead and get your line in." Curtis seemed only mildly aware that his father had nixed the idea. Eagerly he skipped off to the water's edge and swung his pole in a near-expert arc.

"I might regret getting the two of you together," Cole told her after Curtis was out of earshot. "I can see now that it might turn out to be a case of what one won't think of, the other one will."

Veronica's gaze shifted from Cole's grinning expression to the sight of the small boy fishing on the bank. She was unaware of the look of faint longing in her eyes.

"Am I going to stick this poor helpless worm, or not?" she asked him suddenly. The wistful look had disappeared. Cole stared at her for a few uncomfortable moments before he answered.

"You've got too much worm there, Ronnie. You'll have to break him in half."

Veronica's face was incredulous. "Do you mean I'll have to...?"

"'Fraid so," Cole answered. Then holding out his hand, he said, "I'll do it."

"I'll do it myself," she replied. "You and Curtis came up here to enjoy fishing, not bait hooks for a squeamish female." She gritted her teeth and performed the unpleasant but necessary task.

Cole chuckled. "I'm glad to see that little tomboy is still in there somewhere underneath that quiet reserve of yours, Veronica." His low rough voice brought her attention back to his face. "It would be a real shame if she couldn't come out and play with the boys once in a while." Cole's kiss was swift and set his hat askew. He just barely caught it before it fell to the ground.

Moments later, Cole was giving Veronica a few pointers about fishing, teaching her how to cast hook and bait into a deeper part of the lake.

"Dad always says that a good fisherman cleans his own fish." Curtis giggled.

"Someone should have mentioned that earlier," Veronica commented wryly as she glanced across the large flat rock into Cole's laughing eyes. The three of them were sharing the same rock, and soon each was busily cleaning and scaling their catch. The elation

Veronica had felt at catching four fish to Cole's and Curtis's two had definitely tapered off now that she struggled with the task of cleaning what she'd caught.

It wasn't so bad, really, she'd decided, but she hoped her appetite for fried fish wouldn't be unduly affected.

Once she had finished the task Cole expertly filleted the fish. Before they left for the campsite, he deposited the scraps in a shallow hole he'd had Curtis dig earlier.

Curtis gathered up their poles and the tackle box, carefully stowing the cup of worms inside the box before he started up the trail ahead of Cole and Veronica. Veronica had all she could manage with her crutches and Cole followed her with the large plastic freezer bag of fillets, giving her an occasional hand up over a steep spot on the trail.

The afternoon had been idyllic. The three of them had fished companionably the entire time, with Curtis jabbering to them both despite Cole's chuckling reminders that he would scare off the fish. Veronica was thrilled that the boy spoke to her nearly as often as he did to his father. There had been no trace of inhibition or inkling of the reason for his mistrust and fear of her the other day.

At Veronica's insistence, Cole had agreed to stop questioning his son about the incident at Helen's. Apparently, if today was any indication, it had been the right thing to do and Veronica felt untold satisfaction. They were almost at the campsite when they heard Curtis's whoop of excitement.

"Uncle Bob!"

Veronica heard Cole growl something under his breath, and they both increased their pace as the path grew level. Now they could hear the sound of tent stakes being

driven into the hard ground. Cole and Veronica stepped
into the clearing just in time to see Curtis launch himself
into Jessica Ryan's welcoming arms.

CHAPTER ELEVEN

"HEY, DAD! Look who's here!"

Curtis was behaving as if he hadn't seen Jessie and his aunt and uncle for months instead of just the day before. Bob and Wylie, who'd come along too, were nearly finished setting up one of their tents, and Helen and Jessie had already unfolded a large camping table and carried most of their gear to the campsite across the stone ring from Cole's tent.

"What is all this, Helen?" Cole's voice was deceptively soft, but Veronica could almost feel its underlying hardness.

"We were coming up the trail on our way to that site north of here—you know the one—" Helen explained, as if she hadn't noticed her brother-in-law's annoyance. "Well, we saw your truck and decided to join you and Curtis. We didn't think you'd mind." Helen managed to look just worried enough about Cole's reception of their intrusion to bring a resigned twist to his lips, then a more sociable smile.

"Ronnie and I were about to start supper."

It was only then that Helen's eyes moved from Cole to Veronica.

"And you have Veronica with you." Helen's pleased expression rang false to Veronica, and from the look Cole shot her, it had to him, too. "Well..." Helen glanced around to catch her husband's attention. "Bob? Maybe you won't need to set up the tent. You men can bunk in with Cole and Curtis, and the girls and I will use our tent."

"No. Put up the other tent, Bob," Cole called, his cool gaze never leaving Helen's. "Ronnie and I already have all the chaperoning we need," Cole responded casually as he set the bag of fish on the small table he'd brought, then went off to the truck for the other food. Veronica managed a polite smile at the interlopers, hoping their arrival didn't signal a premature end to the happy relaxed atmosphere of the camping trip.

CURTIS HAD BEEN ASLEEP for at least an hour and Veronica had gone to her tent soon after, changing out of her clothing and shrugging into a thigh-length T-shirt nightie. She was still uncomfortable with the tension that had all but ruined the evening for her, and she lay awake listening to the sounds outside. The others hadn't gone to bed yet, but the talk around the fire dwindled to near silence when Cole decided to retire for the night. She noticed through the small nylon mesh window that the light in Cole's neighboring tent was now off. She could hear the others bidding goodnight to each other, and then, almost suddenly, all was quiet.

Just as Veronica was drifting off to sleep, a shuffling sound outside her tent summoned her back to complete consciousness. She could hear the low buzzing sound of the double zipper at the door flap and sensed Cole's presence in the darkness even before he leaned over to crawl inside her tent, zipping the flap closed behind him. She felt a thrill of excitement when he gently touched her shoulder.

"Ronnie, are you awake?" he whispered, crouching beside her.

"Yes," she whispered back. "What are you doing here, Cole? What will the others think . . . and Curtis?"

"Shh." He placed a finger gently over her lips, his eyes now nearly adjusted to the blackness. "Curtis is sound asleep. If there's a problem, we're right next door, and I'll be back there before he's awake. As for the others, I don't care what they think."

"Cole, I—"

"Ronnie, I'd just like to lie close to you for a while." The words wrapped irresistibly around her heart and she whispered her consent. Cole eased himself onto the edge of Veronica's bedroll, sliding beneath the blankets to stretch his length alongside hers.

"I'm sorry about tonight, Ronnie. I had no idea Helen and Jessie would pull something like this." Cole's whisper was harsh.

"You don't need to apologize," Veronica whispered back.

She wanted to end the conversation there. She didn't think she could keep from commenting on several barbed remarks Jessie had made that evening, or the way Helen never missed an opportunity to link Cole's name with Jessie's. Wylie had been short-tempered—and with cause, Veronica thought sympathetically. He had apparently been counting on a cozy little trip with Jessie, but Jessie had obviously used him so she would have someone to toss in Veronica's direction while she went after Cole.

Veronica felt the subtle tension next to her escalate just before she heard a stirring of movement as Cole reached for her in the darkness. She didn't resist when he drew her close and rearranged the blankets until they were sharing one another's warmth.

Slowly, hesitantly, as if giving her a chance to refuse, Cole's lips found the shell of her ear. The hard arm that encircled her waist began to move upward as his gentle fingers found the neckline of her nightie and tugged it aside to bare her shoulder to his kiss. With a distinct absence of haste, Cole slipped his other hand beneath her head, pillowing her on his forearm as he turned her onto her back and found her lips. As she felt herself begin to melt, Veronica's arms went around Cole's neck in unreserved invitation.

A tremor shot through her when Cole thrust his tongue forcefully into her mouth while his hand found the hem of her night shirt. With a riveting mixture of laziness and determination, Cole stroked her thigh, then let his hand wander up to her hip and across her flat stomach before moving higher. In moments, Veronica was feverishly returning Cole's kiss, going breathless when he slipped a jeans-clad leg between her thighs and shifted more and more of his weight onto her smallness.

Her night shirt slid higher as Cole's warm sure fingers toyed enticingly with her breast. The heat beneath the blankets became sweltering as Cole's lips left hers to burrow beneath the ripple of clothing and find the small hardened peak.

Suddenly there was a cry from Curtis's tent.

"Look at this fish, Dad," the childish voice called out.

Cole went as still as if he'd heard a shot, and Veronica's pleasure-tormented gasp died in her throat. The only sound for startled moments was the rapid staccato of two racing hearts as they listened for more.

"See him?" they heard Curtis say.

Cole carefully smoothed Veronica's night shirt down over her hips.

"What'd I tell ya?" the happy little voice chattered, and Veronica began to shake with silent laughter.

"Talking in his sleep," Cole whispered unnecessarily before he, too, started to chuckle. "Let me make a quick check on him. I'll be right back."

He rose and moved toward the tent entrance, then exited and looked in on his son. After watching him roll over and lie in silence for a few minutes, Cole decided the sleep chatter must be finished.

"I guess we couldn't ask for a better chaperon than a seven-year-old boy," Cole said as he made his way back into Veronica's tent. He started planting skin-branding kisses on her neck, but Veronica sensed his self-control was back in place.

Suddenly Cole said, "I think I'm falling for you, Veronica."

Veronica's rapidly beating heart skidded to a halt at the unexpected words. A warmth came into her, a free-flowing, heart-bursting heat that crested deep inside, yet left her with a bittersweet ache.

Careful, her mind cautioned. Cole's very choice of words was a clear intimation that he was still unsure of what he really felt. He *thought* he was falling for her, she reminded herself. That was still eons away from a simple heartfelt "I love you, Veronica."

"I care for you, too, Cole," she heard herself say, desperate to sound casual and unaffected. "But I'm really tired. I'd like to get some sleep now." She started to roll out of Cole's arms and pull away from him when his arms tightened almost fiercely around her.

"You can't just turn over and go to sleep!" Cole's whispered rasp was incredulous.

Veronica kept silent, staring up into the shadow of Cole's face. She couldn't see him clearly, but she could almost feel the harsh line of his mouth. In another moment Cole relaxed his hold and Veronica took the opportunity to turn away from him.

Although she was reluctant to abandon the whipcord length that warmed her back, she managed to summon the strength to shift away from Cole to the far edge of the rumpled bedroll.

"You don't have to go, Ronnie," came the near-silent whisper. Veronica paused, feeling the emotional tentacles of his words wrap around her and tug at her resistance. Her mind raced frantically for a way to escape Cole's persuasion.

"Playing around with you like this can only lead to one thing," she whispered irritably. Veronica drew the blankets to her chin as she lay on her side and stared at the blackened tent side.

"So?"

Veronica sighed then pulled her knees up to lie in a defensive curl, wondering what she should say. What *could* she say? Was it time to tell Cole everything about her marriage to Eric? Or would there ever be an appropriate time? Did Cole even care to know? Maybe, she thought, there was really no reason to tell him anything. Veronica squeezed her eyes shut, electing to sleep and say nothing.

"It's your husband, isn't it?" Veronica's eyes popped open. "Or rather, ex-husband."

The silence of the night had grown unbearably loud. The sounds of the forest around them had paused, as if waiting for her to respond. Suddenly, it all seemed a secret not worth keeping. The months since the accident felt like years, the agony of Eric's abandonment no longer the raw wound it had been.

"I don't still love him, if that's what you mean," she said quietly.

"Is that why you divorced him?" came the inevitable question.

Veronica made a restless movement. "Is this just idle curiosity, or do you really want to know about my marriage to Eric?" Cole didn't hesitate.

"There are things you do, things you've said, that raise a lot of questions, Ronnie. So yes, I'd really like to know about your marriage."

Veronica started slowly, telling Cole only a few things at first about her relationship with Eric—the wedding, the accident, but including enough so he'd know that her sexual inexperience was total.

Veronica was able to relax then and found herself confiding her heartache that after his first visit, Eric had never been back to the hospital to see her and that he'd had their marriage annulled soon after. She even mentioned the personally unattractive part about sinking into depression for weeks, resisting anyone who tried to help her.

When she finished, Veronica lay quietly, her heart emptied of emotion, cleansed of the fear of humiliation that had lingered inside her for months.

"I survived," she whispered, aware of the awkwardness Cole must be feeling.

There was a rustling movement and Cole was suddenly propped on an elbow. Veronica turned her head and stared up at the breathing shadow that hovered over her and waited. She felt Cole's warm breath on her face the instant before his lips settled on hers. There was no passion in his kiss, only a gentle, compassionate, coaxing kind of contact.

"I'm sorry, baby," came the velvet whisper. Veronica didn't resist as Cole turned her to face him, then drew her close.

This time, she lay facing him, cradled against his lean length by strong arms. Neither spoke as Veronica snuggled deeper into Cole's embrace, feeling at peace with herself. The warmth and strength Cole's body offered was like heaven, the broad, hair-roughened chest she was cuddled against tantalizingly male. With the warm wonderful scent of him in her nostrils, Veronica gradually found sleep, comforted by the complete trust she now felt toward him.

FOR THE TENTH TIME in the past half hour Veronica glanced out the kitchen window, checking to see where Curtis was. Something about the way he was acting today distressed her. He had been sullen and uncommunicative since the day after they'd returned from the camping trip, but Veronica was hard put to pinpoint the reason.

The camping trip itself had turned out a success. After a very early quick breakfast that Helen and Jessie had insisted on preparing, the two women packed a huge lunch for the hike they assumed Bob and Wylie were taking on their own. Minutes after the lunches were loaded into backpacks, Helen and Jessie found, to their dismay, that they were expected to go along. Cole's frosty demeanor discouraged either of them from finding excuses to stay behind.

With the two women thwarted for the remainder of the day, Cole and Veronica had spent most of their time fishing with Curtis. At first, Veronica was uncomfortable when Cole used every opportunity to touch her, regardless of whether Curtis was watching or not. But gradually, Curtis stopped making faces of revulsion every time he saw his father kiss her. He even parked himself and his fishing pole next to them on the bank while Veronica sat on the ground in front of Cole, leaning back companionably against his chest.

By the time they packed up their tent and camping supplies to head for home, anyone seeing the three of them together might have assumed they were a family. That was probably the reason, when Helen and Jessie trudged back to the campsite behind Bob and Wylie, that the two footsore, whining women's every look indicated they would surely set another plan in action to disrupt the newly bonded threesome. Now that plan, if one did exist, seemed to be working.

Veronica pushed the door open and walked out onto the porch, aided by the walking cane that the therapist had recommended she begin using after her last visit. Unable to see Curtis anywhere out back, she carefully descended the porch steps and headed toward the side of the house. Just as she rounded the end of the porch, the charred smell of burning paper assailed her nostrils.

"What are you doing, Curtis?" Veronica bent at the waist, her hand braced on the porch rail for balance, to peer under the porch. Her quiet approach had been missed by the boy who was scrambling to toss clumps of earth on the tiny pile of shredded newsprint he'd just touched a match to. "Come out from under there."

Round-eyed, Curtis obeyed the calm order without question.

"Give me the matches." Veronica put out her hand, silently debating the best way to handle the situation. Cole wouldn't be home for at least a couple of hours, and Veronica was still uncertain how far he expected her to go in disciplining the boy. Curtis's face was filled with mutiny as he dropped a single matchbook into her out-stretched palm. "Is that all of them?"

A dusty sneaker speared the sod. "Yep."

"I'm surprised at this, Curtis," Veronica began, feeling her way with the boy, not liking that she had to further risk his resentment. "You know how dangerous fires can be."

The sneakered toe twisted. "You gonna tell my dad?" Curtis's small chin came up at a defiant angle.

"I think one of us should tell him, don't you?" Curtis's lower lip quivered and Veronica had to harden herself to the boy's distress. "Why don't you run into the house and get a pitcher of water? The plastic one on the counter next to the sink will do fine."

"Why?" Again that challenging lift of chin.

"I want you to make sure that the fire is properly doused," Veronica explained patiently.

"It was just some paper," Curtis protested, and Veronica saw definite signs of Jessie in his shrugging, faintly ridiculing attitude.

"Are you going to mind me, or do you want to spend the afternoon in your room?" Veronica uttered the ultimatum with unwavering calm, trying to remember what she'd read about offering children options like that. The experts often disagreed, so Veronica had little to draw on but her own childhood experience. Unfortunately, as she recalled a bit belatedly, the problem adults had usually run into with her was that she almost always chose the punishment.

"Oh, all right," Curtis grumbled, then reached for the porch rail to climb onto the end of the porch like the half boy, half monkey he was. In a few minutes, he was carrying the pitcher out the back door, choosing the more conventional stairs before he came around the porch toward her. Veronica leaned down and watched as Curtis spilled the water over the powder-fine remains before he crawled back out.

"Thank you, Curtis." Veronica took the pitcher. "I've been baking cookies this afternoon," she said in a brighter tone. "How would you like to sample some?" She was grateful to be able to have something to offer that would let Curtis know she was still willing to be friendly despite the problems.

"I saw 'em. I even tasted one," he replied, almost as if he were daring her to tell him he shouldn't have.

"That's all right," she assured him. "Why not come in and have a big glass of milk with some more?" Veronica took heart at the sudden waver in the boy's defiant expression.

"Because I didn't like 'em," he burst out, then raced past her toward the trees at the edge of the yard. Veronica watched him go, hurt by his refusal.

"Your father wants you to stay in the yard," she called after him, then, disheartened, started for the porch steps.

The tentative acceptance Curtis had shown on their trip had vanished. If anything, the boy seemed more intolerant of her than ever. He'd spent Monday and Tuesday at Helen's, but Cole had kept him home the rest of the week, asking Veronica if she minded keeping an eye on him the few times he couldn't take Curtis with him around the ranch.

Yet in spite of Cole's almost too-obvious machinations to give her and Curtis more opportunity to get to know each other, Curtis remained withdrawn from her, unless he found something to criticize.

That had led her to suspect that Helen had possibly had a hand in the boy's sudden reversal. Things had been fine between Veronica and Curtis until he'd come home

Tuesday afternoon, and there hadn't been a truly relaxed moment with him since. It upset Veronica that Helen could be so vindictive.

And really there was little point in Helen's being so, for Cole's interest in Veronica was just a passing thing, she was sure. She had likely come along at the time when Cole was finally ready to stop mourning Jackie and think about a new relationship. Even though Veronica was head over heels in love with Cole, she didn't delude herself into thinking his feelings matched the intensity of hers. It hurt to remind herself that every look, every touch, every kiss and every confidence they shared would eventually come to nothing. Veronica had no illusions about her ability to sustain Cole's romantic interest. She only hoped that when that interest did wane, she could anticipate it and take the initiative to end their relationship by quietly slipping out of Cole's life.

With these depressing thoughts on her mind, Veronica made her way to the freezer to choose what meat to set out to thaw for the next day. She was just about to remove a roast of beef when she heard a scream from the back yard.

Grabbing her cane, Veronica turned and rushed awkwardly outside, hitting the porch door and sending it banging against the house as she did so. The horror that met her eyes when her frantic gaze found Curtis next to the barbecue grill made her grab the throw rug that lay across the porch rail. Fear propelled her still weak and unsteady legs rapidly down the steps, and she was heedless of the jarring pain that rocketed through her limbs to her hips and backbone.

In moments she reached Curtis. He was doing a wild kicking dance that served only to spread the hungry blaze of fire from his right sneaker to the ankle of his jeans.

Veronica half lunged and half fell to drag the boy to the ground, smothering the flames with the small rug. Curtis writhed with pain as she tried to gauge the extent and severity of the burns that had eaten away at the top of his shoe and crept up past the hem of his jeans.

"Shorty!" Veronica's yell was directed toward the barns where Shorty usually spent a good part of the afternoon. She held Curtis tightly, her heart wrenching at the sight of his small tearless face, pale as he stared up at her in a mute plea for reassurance.

"You'll be all right, sweetheart," she crooned. "We'll get you to the doctor right away. Shorty!"

"I want my dad," Curtis whispered, and Veronica hugged him even closer.

"We'll get him. Don't worry." Veronica didn't have time to wonder how they would reach Cole. Shorty raced over from the barn, his weathered face whitening at the sight of Veronica on the ground, cradling Curtis.

"Lord a mercy! What'd he do, get hisself burnt?" Shorty was already swooping down to whisk the boy into his arms.

"Get him to the car and see if you can get his shoe off. Then elevate his foot, Shorty," Veronica ordered. "Can we take the station wagon?" She reached for her cane and rose painfully to her feet. Teddy, who'd just arrived on the scene, came close to steady her. "Teddy?" She barely noticed that the small fire was licking across the dry grass of the yard or that Jim Fisher was running from the barn with a feed sack to beat it out. "Get three of those bags of ice out of the freezer and grab a sheet out of the linen closet."

"Can you make it to the car okay?" Teddy's gentle brown eyes were worried.

"Yes. I'm fine. Please hurry." Reluctantly he released her and ran to the house. Veronica forced her aching legs toward the old station wagon where Shorty had deposited Curtis. Just as she reached the wagon, Teddy emerged from the house with the bags of ice and the sheet. Hampered by leg cramps that threatened to draw her thigh muscles into knots, Veronica climbed into the rear of the wagon. She partially unfolded the sheet and slid it beneath Curtis's injured foot, which Shorty had managed to free from the burned shoe and rest on a tool box. Frantic fingers tore open the plastic ice bags, gently packing the ice on and around the boy's foot and ankle before she wrapped the soothing cold securely with the sheet. Curtis whimpered during her ministrations but didn't pull away, and in moments Teddy had climbed behind the wheel of the car and got it started.

"I'll see if'n I can raise Cole on the CB," Shorty said, poking his head into the wagon. "If'n I can't, I'll go find him."

"Good. But call Helen first and ask her to come to the hospital. Curtis may feel better if she's there. Then call the hospital to let them know we're coming." Veronica was unaware that her hands were trembling.

"Will do. You two take care." Shorty smiled encouragingly at the small boy who managed a quirk of lips before the old cowhand closed the tailgate securely.

Teddy gunned the engine and they shot down the driveway while Veronica held Curtis's hand. The boy clung to her, bravely trying to hold back tears.

OUTSIDE THE TRAUMA ROOM at the hospital, Veronica waited nervously, her lower body enveloped in a relentless ache. But the ache in her heart was far greater. She had let Cole down, violated the trust he'd put in her. And now Curtis lay in pain just beyond that door because of her negligence.

Veronica doubted she'd ever forget the anguish and fear in those so solemn little eyes, a look that had gripped her soul and brought every mothering instinct she possessed to the surface. During the ride to the hospital she had held Curtis's hand, stroked his forehead, and spoken reassuringly to him, frustrated that she could do no more to comfort him or take away his pain.

But the instant Helen had come through the trauma-room door, Curtis had shrugged off Veronica's touch and reached for his aunt. Helen had hugged the boy, her curt "You can go back to the ranch, Veronica—I'm here now" effectively dismissing Veronica from the room.

Veronica remained in the hall, leaning against the wall to take some stress off her legs. She waited almost fearfully for Cole to arrive. Teddy had gone back to the ranch when a quick call home told him that Shorty still hadn't been able to track down Cole. Veronica had no way of getting back to the ranch, but even if she had, she wouldn't think of leaving. Not until she was certain Curtis would be all right.

Veronica's stomach twisted with guilt, her mind incapable of formulating thoughts that didn't begin with "If only..." If only she'd watched Curtis more closely. If only she'd paid more attention when he'd come into the kitchen that last time. If only she'd noticed he'd taken the can of charcoal lighter fluid from beneath the sink when she'd pulled out a new garbage bag. If only...

"What's happened to Curtis?"

Veronica turned, startled by the angry demand in Jessica Ryan's voice.

"He was playing with matches and had some charcoal lighter fluid out by the grill. He must have spilled some on his foot and it ignited when he struck a match."

"How bad is he?"

"He's burned his foot and ankle, but I'm not certain how badly. The doctor is in there now and Helen is with him," Veronica answered, brushing the dampness from her pale cheek. "Shorty hasn't been able to reach Cole yet." Jessie's cloudy look darkened.

"Well, you've done it this time," Jessie jeered, a slim hand waving in the air in an I-told-you-so gesture. "Cole should have known better than to let you look after Curtis." Jessie rearranged the angry lines of her face into a satisfied smile. "If I were you, I think I'd be getting out of town on the next bus, train, or plane going anyplace far, far from here. I don't think I'd even go back to the ranch for my toothbrush."

Veronica looked away guiltily, only able to think about the obvious parallel between Curtis's accident and Chapman Red's all those years ago. She'd been at least indirectly at fault both times, the blame resting on her irresponsible behavior.

"I warned you about history repeating itself, didn't I?" Jessie needled.

Veronica felt cold and sick, smothered by the escalation of the guilt she'd already assigned herself. She was terrified of facing Cole now, but face him she must. She deserved everything he'd have to say to the person who had violated his trust and allowed his only child to come to harm.

"I can't leave, Jessie," she murmured, then turned away from the lovely blonde whose perfect face tightened unpleasantly.

"You can't be thinking to talk your way out of this, are you?" Jessie's voice was filled with scorn. Neither of them noticed the trauma-room door opening only to be pushed almost—but not quite—closed again.

"Do you honestly think," Jessie went on, "that just because Cole seems to have developed some kind of passing interest in you that he'll overlook your negligence?" She laughed. "Not a chance, Veronica. He'll be out for blood, and this time Hank won't be around to protect you. Cole will hang you out to dry."

Veronica took a quick breath.

"Then I guess that's the way it will be," she whispered, feeling as if she deserved to be hung out to dry.

"Look, Veronica," Jessie persisted, "this is not at all like what happened to Red. Oh, I suppose in some ways it is," she conceded when Veronica glanced back at her. "But you and I both know you didn't forget to properly secure that damned horse," she said with a toss of her head. "This time, Curtis was in your care and you failed to keep an eye on him." Veronica turned then, unable to put her finger on what Jessie was saying, but alert to it. "You really are a naive little sap, aren't you?"

"What?"

"You're a naive little sap," Jessie repeated as if she enjoyed saying it.

"No. The other. About you and I both knowing I didn't forget to secure Chapman Red." Veronica's eyes narrowed. "You were the one who reminded Cole that the two of you had just seen me coming from Red's paddock. I always thought you believed I was at fault."

In fact, Veronica recalled, Jessie had been the one who had incited Cole's volatile temper and goaded him on, feeding the fire of his anger toward Veronica. It came as a shock to hear that Jessie had actually believed, *known*, otherwise. Why hadn't she said so at the time?

"I knew you weren't," Jessie dismissed with a flourish of her hand.

"Then why didn't you say so?"

"Are you really so dense, Veronica? Why should I have? After I went to all the trouble of turning Red out myself, why shouldn't I have made certain you were blamed?" Jessie was untroubled by Veronica's gasp. "I was hoping for better results, though. Especially after that stupid horse had to be put down. I'd hoped old Hank would turn against you then, too, so I wouldn't have to worry about him throwing you at Cole one day. He was always so damned determined for Cole to like you."

Jessie smirked as Veronica's jaw dropped in astonishment.

"You did it deliberately, then blamed me?" Veronica was trembling. "You let me think all these years that I'd..." Veronica stared, incredulous. "My God, Jessie. How could you have destroyed a valuable animal like that? Cole loved that horse."

"Cole could have any horse he wanted. What was the loss of one horse when I had such a great opportunity to ruin your chances with Cole forever?"

"But I was sixteen years old, Jessie. I wasn't any threat to you, and Cole couldn't even stand to have me around. Besides, he was in love with Jackie."

"You're right about that," Jessie admitted ruefully. "Jackie could do no wrong as far as Cole was concerned. I never could think of a way to come between them before they were married. But when Jackie died so conveniently, I promised myself that no other woman was going to be the next Mrs. Cole Chapman but me.

That's why I've got so close to Curtis," she went on. "I have him wrapped so tightly around my little finger that I almost have him believing you're a two-headed monster from the nether world." Jessie's laughter was cold.

"You used the boy?" Veronica felt sick. No wonder Curtis had been so hostile and frightened of her.

"Of course," Jessie readily confessed. "Remember the day Curtis refused to ride home in the car with you from Helen's?" Jessie chuckled at Veronica's look of confusion. "I told Curtis you were the one driving six months ago when you had your accident. I said you were a very bad driver."

"But that's not true," Veronica cried.

"Curtis thinks so," Jessie reminded her. "And the fact that Curtis and I are buddies made it easy for me to persuade him to keep quiet and not tell Cole." Jessie's smile was almost sinister. "And now, thanks to Curtis's timely little accident, I'm going to be able to keep that promise to myself after all, since you'll be out of the way." A smug look crossed her face. "I still can't figure out what Cole sees in you."

With these words Jessie turned away and walked toward the elevator bank, leaving Veronica in a daze. So Chapman Red's death had been caused by Jessie. The knowledge of the woman's premeditated evil shocked her and forestalled any relief she might have felt at the revelation. And then to hear that Jessie had been manipulating Curtis! No wonder Veronica was having problems with the boy.

Yet how ironic it was that Jessie was accepted and championed by Cole's unsuspecting sister-in-law. At least Veronica assumed Helen didn't know—not when Jessie's admission showed such contempt for Jackie and such deliberate exploitation of little Curtis.

Veronica stared at the leggy blonde who was preening before her reflection in the glass of a wall-mounted floor directory near the elevators. Her thoughts were disrupted by the cautious opening of the trauma-room door as Helen stepped into the hall.

"Veronica?" The concerned look Helen was giving her sent a jolt of fear through her, obliterating any thought beyond Curtis's condition.

"How is he, Helen?" Veronica's eyes were haunted, her heart wrenched with anxiety. From the look on Helen's face, Curtis's burns must have been much worse than the doctor had initially thought. *If only I'd watched him more closely,* she again cried to herself.

"Curtis will be all right," Helen said, but the odd look she was giving Veronica indicated differently.

"Are you certain?" Tears of relief coursed down Veronica's pale cheeks and she clumsily reached to dash them away. Helen put out her hand and Veronica flinched, unprepared for Helen's gentle touch of consolation.

Helen started to speak, but just as she did, Veronica was drawn to a flurry of movement down the hall. Cole had burst through the double doors into the emergency entrance. He paused momentarily, his granite expression forbidding, his blue eyes like polished steel as his gaze skipped over Jessica and riveted on Veronica.

Long purposeful strides brought Cole quickly down the hall, and Veronica felt herself begin to tremble. He looked lean and tough, his dusty battered Stetson resting at a dangerous angle over his glittering eyes. Cole reached for her, his iron fingers seizing her upper arms just as her knees threatened to buckle.

CHAPTER TWELVE

VERONICA DREW BACK, throwing her hands up against Cole's chest in self-protection. Then the gentleness of his grip registered. He was leaning down, his raking gaze missing nothing as he searched her pale features.

"Are you all right, Ronnie?" he rasped with concern as he tugged her closer. Veronica nodded, unable to suppress a tiny sob.

"I wouldn't waste my precious time coddling her if it was my son lying in that trauma room suffering." Jessie had followed along the hall and now her icy voice brought his head around. "All that talk that day about Curtis's being safe in the pickup truck meant nothing more to her than a way to keep me from your son. I told you that, Cole. Curtis's safety didn't mean a whole hell of a lot when she couldn't be bothered to notice he was playing with charcoal lighter and matches."

Jessie was the picture of outraged femininity, her face flushed, her eyes accusing, her manicured hands balled into dainty fists that rested on her shapely hips. She fully looked the part of an angry concerned mother—just the image she wanted to project, Veronica realized helplessly.

"Are you Mr. Chapman?" An authoritative male voice cut between them and Cole released Veronica to thrust out his hand to shake the doctor's.

"How's my son?"

"He's a very lucky little boy," the sandy-haired emergency-room doctor declared. Veronica hung on every word as he informed Cole that Curtis's burns were mostly second degree, that the thickness of his socks and sneakers had kept the fire from burning more quickly through to his skin. Then he praised Veronica for applying the ice, because it had alleviated much of Curtis's discomfort. Also, he said, her quick action in smothering the fire had prevented Curtis from getting extensive third-degree burns.

Although relieved that Curtis's condition was not serious and that the doctor had commended her, Veronica's sense of doom increased. Cole had physically withdrawn from her, leaving her to lean exhaustedly on her cane.

He blamed her, she was certain, unable to argue with that because she blamed herself. Veronica experienced a brief spurt of encouragement when Cole turned again to face her, asking her once more if she was all right. Thanking her, he followed the doctor back into the trauma room.

"Why don't we go and sit down?" Helen offered, taking Veronica's arm to coax her to the tiny waiting area nearby. Veronica shook her head and turned away, but not before she caught sight of the smug look on Jessie's face. "Please, Veronica," Helen urged.

Why was Helen being so kind, Veronica wondered, her eyes drawn from Jessie back to Helen.

"Maybe later," she said. "But you go ahead," she hastened to add, then moved unsteadily to a spot where she was within sight of the trauma-room door, but out of the way.

Jessie lost no time in stepping next to Helen, leaning over to whisper conspiratorially when Veronica glanced their way. To her surprise, and evidently to Jessie's by the look on her face, Helen walked away from the blond woman in midsentence. Jessie stood open-mouthed for a second, then hurried after her friend.

Veronica continued to watch only because this was a clear departure from the norm in Helen and Jessie's relationship. She could have sworn the two women were close friends, but Helen's expression was closed, her whole manner discouraging further talk on Jessie's part.

Veronica looked away, forcing herself to watch the activity in the hall, wishing she had a more absorbing distraction from the guilt and apprehension she felt. Mercifully she wasn't kept in suspense much longer.

The trauma-room door swung open wide and Cole emerged, followed by the doctor. After a brief leave-taking and another handshake, Cole's gaze sped to Veronica. She tried to discern what would happen next as she watched him move toward her in his loose-jointed cowboy walk. Visibly shaken, Cole stopped and let his eyes sweep over her.

The time that passed while Veronica waited for Cole's ashen expression to switch to rage seemed frightfully long to her, but was only the blink of an eyelash to anyone else. Any moment he would explode the way he did eight years earlier. Knowing now that Red's death hadn't been her fault did nothing to dim the memory, and Veronica stood bravely, waiting for the inevitable.

Suddenly she was in Cole's arms, his lips moving over her cheek as he placed possessive kisses on her pale skin.

"I'm so sorry, Cole," Veronica murmured. "It was all my fault. I thought I'd gotten all the matches—" Veronica's voice broke on a sob, heartsick that Curtis was hurting. The steellike arms tightened, pulling her small body even more firmly against him.

"It's not your fault, dammit," he growled into her ear, then planted a kiss on her wet cheek. He straightened slightly, pinning her weeping gaze with the anguished blue of his own. "But you expected me to jump all over you, that right?" Cole's expression revealed that her fear and uncertainty of him had hurt. "Damn." He hugged her fiercely. "I trust you completely, Ronnie, especially with my son. The way you handled this whole crisis only reinforces my faith in you."

Veronica's heart leaped into a joyous rapid cadence as Cole continued to hold her.

"Mr. Chapman?" The nurse stood a couple feet away from where they stood in each other's arms, but Cole only loosened his embrace enough to turn his head toward the white-clad woman. "You can go back in with Curtis now," she said. "It will be a few minutes before he's ready to go upstairs."

"Thank you, nurse." Cole faced Veronica again, releasing her slowly. "Did you hurt yourself?" he asked, looking at her legs.

"A little," Veronica admitted. "But it's nothing that some liniment and a couple of heating pads won't cure. Don't worry about me." Veronica wanted him to hurry in to his son and not waste time with her. Curtis needed his father.

"Come on." Cole stepped back only enough to signal that she was to precede him. "Curtis was asking to see you." Veronica hesitated, surprised. "Come on," Cole repeated and Veronica brushed away any lingering dampness from her cheeks, glancing up at Cole in silent question. Grinning, Cole reached into his hip pocket and brought out a garish red handkerchief, which he used to tenderly wipe the wet wedges of mascara from beneath her lashes. They were nearly to the trauma-room door when Jessie stepped into their path.

"Excuse us, Jessie." Cole's hard arm brusquely swept the blond woman aside without giving her a chance to speak. "Ronnie's going in to see Curtis." The door swished closed behind Veronica, muffling the sound of Jessie's instant objection.

Veronica stared at the small sheet-covered form on the gurney, smiling when Curtis's solemn gray eyes found hers. She started across the tiled floor hesitantly.

"You hurt your legs." The child's words were more a statement than a question.

Veronica shrugged. "I just overworked a couple of muscles. No damage done. How are you feeling?" Veronica stopped at Curtis's side, glancing at the nurse who hovered nearby taking the boy's blood pressure.

Curtis didn't look too comfortable and Veronica reached for the small hand that rested on the side rail, curling her fingers consolingly around it.

"I hurt a little," he admitted, and Veronica hoped they had given him something for the pain he must have surely felt. "I just wish I didn't do what I done."

"I guess you learned an awfully hard lesson," she whispered, nearly overcome with compassion. Not only had he been hurt, he'd probably been scared to death. "I'm sorry I didn't catch you before you lit the match."

Curtis's eyes fled from contact with hers. "You weren't supposed to catch me. I snuck the lighter fluid out when you went into the bathroom." Curtis's eyes brimmed with tears. "But I'll never do it again. Fire hurts." Veronica gripped the side rail and snapped it down, leaning over to give Curtis a hug.

"Oh, sweetheart, I'm so sorry you're hurting." To her surprise and heart-bursting pleasure, Curtis's arms hooked around her neck and pulled her closer. She held on to him until he loosened his arms and withdrew.

"Dad said I should tell you I'm sorry." Curtis's words revealed that what had just happened between them had been unintentional on his part and he wasn't quite comfortable about it.

"I'll accept your apology, Curtis, on the promise you'll do everything the doctors and nurses tell you so you can hurry home. It's going to be hard on your father for the two of you to be apart too long." The boy seemed to brighten a bit at that. "We're all going to miss you," she added sincerely.

"Okay," Curtis readily agreed.

Veronica glanced at the nurse who nodded in response to her unspoken question. "I guess I've got to go now, Curtis. Is there anything we can bring from home for you?"

"Dad and Aunt Helen know already."

"All right. I'll see you after you get up to your room." She smiled down at him, then started to turn away.

"Veronica?"

Veronica turned back to the boy, who looked so small and vulnerable.

"If you wouldn't mind, I'd like some of those cookies you baked." Curtis blushed, then glanced at the nurse to see if she was listening, but she seemed totally absorbed in making notations on his chart. "I only pretended not to like them," he confessed. "Would you?"

"Of course I will." Veronica's smile broadened. "You concentrate on getting well, okay?"

Curtis's little mouth curved. "Okay."

Elated, Veronica went back out into the hall.

"I'm not going to argue with you about it, Jess," Cole was saying. "Maybe it's time you made an attempt to make up to Veronica. This feud between the two of you has lasted long enough.''

"You can't be serious, Cole," Jessie scoffed. "How can you even suggest that when you know what she's like? If the incident with Chapman Red wasn't bad enough, then surely what happened to Curtis today should have convinced you. You can't mean to keep her around.''

Veronica stared at Jessie, frozen, chilled by Jessie's unrelenting determination to drive a wedge between her and Cole. Veronica suddenly knew she couldn't listen to any more of Jessie's vindictiveness. She was about to edge away when Helen stepped close, her slim brunette form positioned between her brother-in-law and her best friend.

"There are a few things you ought to know, Cole," Helen began, and Veronica glanced away from the look Helen tossed in her direction, certain she was about to lend her influence to the unpleasant discussion.

"First of all, it was Jessie who was responsible for Chapman Red's injury, not Veronica." Jessie's mouth dropped open, her eyes widening on the woman she thought was her closest ally. Cole's gaze had narrowed on both women while Veronica just stared, incredulous. "From what I overheard just a little while ago, I'm afraid it was premeditated, Cole. Jessie apparently planned for Veronica to be blamed.''

Helen paused, then looked directly at Jessie. "I also understand that Jessie has been manipulating Curtis, persuading him into disliking, even being frightened of Veronica." The look Helen was giving Jessie was one of contempt. "There are a few other details—" her gaze flicked back to Cole "—but I think you've heard enough for now.''

"How dare you?" Jessie challenged, her fingers curving like claws, as if she was seriously contemplating scratching out Helen's eyes.

"Is what Helen's saying true?" Cole's jaw was like iron, his eyes diamond hard. Veronica shuddered, knowing all too well how frightening it was to have that near-wild look focused on her.

"I love you, Cole," Jessie stated simply, as if that explained and excused everything. "I'd do anything for you, you know that. But there have been times when you've been...distracted. I had to do something to get you back on the right path again. If I can keep you from making another mistake like Jackie, I will." The delicately pointed chin came up in defiance.

"Mistake?" Cole's voice was deceptively quiet.

"Jackie was all wrong for you, Cole." Jessie laid a proprietorial hand on his thickly muscled forearm. "She had too many ambitions that had nothing to do with you or the ranch. I on the other hand am perfectly willing to devote myself to you. I think I've more than proved that."

Veronica felt a surge of pity for Jessie. She didn't seem to see that what she'd done eight years ago and what she'd tried to pull with Curtis was more than marginally wrong. To her, the end justified the means. Indeed, in Jessie's mind the lengths she had gone to merely proved her love for Cole.

Veronica's eyes shifted from Jessie to Helen then to Cole. Neither Helen nor Cole seemed to be feeling a particle of the pity she felt for the misguided Jessica.

"What kind of woman are you?" Cole breathed. Fear flashed across Jessie's worried expression.

"Jessie was only eighteen at the time, Cole," Veronica put in, instinctively wanting him to treat Jessie gently. Obviously the woman was deranged.

"The thought that an eighteen-year-old is capable of what you did, Jessie, sickens me." Cole's lip curled faintly. "Aside from your callous disregard for the pain and suffering of an animal, you made Veronica suffer damage to her reputation and untold emotional distress." Cole angrily shook off the manicured hand that had started to clutch at his arm.

"And you would have let all of us go on thinking that Veronica was responsible, wouldn't you? If Ronnie hadn't come back..." Cole took a deep breath. "And then using my son.... I trusted you with him." Cole's brow furrowed deeply as Jessie's face drew into an unattractive scowl. "And you aren't sorry, are you?" he stated with dawning perception.

Jessie started to agree, but clamped her mouth shut. The only indication that Cole was right was the unconscious dip of her chin.

Cole's expression suddenly turned to flint, his jaw set. "Curtis and I won't be wanting any more to do with you, Jessie, and I'd appreciate it if you didn't test me on that."

"But Cole—"

"I mean it, Jessie. I can't speak for Helen, but if I ever catch you on my ranch or within shouting distance of Curtis or Veronica again..." Cole's jaw flexed, hardened to the frantic look on Jessie's face as she burst into incredulous tears.

"But, Cole..."

He turned to Veronica, his gentle touch on her elbow signaling her to leave with him.

"Cole?" The blonde seized his arm but Cole brushed her hand away as he would have a pesky fly. "Veronica isn't right for you, Cole," Jessie called after them, desperation giving her voice a high keening quality.

Veronica shot a worried sideways look at Cole, but the glitter of rage in his eyes forestalled any thought of persuading him to be a bit more merciful to Jessie. In spite of what Jessie had done, Veronica felt sorry for her. When Helen fell into step on the other side of Cole, Veronica realized that she was wasting no sorrow on her former friend, either.

IT WAS LATER, after they'd grabbed a cup of coffee in the cafeteria, then gone upstairs to make certain Curtis was settled in his room for the night, that the three of them left the hospital. They were in the parking lot beside Helen's car when Helen spoke.

"I can't begin to tell you how sorry I am for the way I've treated you, Veronica. I guess I've been suffering from a particularly bad case of stupidity."

"I understand, Helen," Veronica said sincerely. "It's all right."

"No, it's not all right," the brunette said vehemently. "I've been unforgivably rude and ungracious to you."

"It's all right—really," Veronica assured her. "I'd feel more comfortable if we'd both just forget about it." Veronica had no problem managing a smile, pleased when Helen's worried look slackened and she allowed herself to smile back.

"Thank you, Veronica," Helen said, then hesitated. "I'd really like it if we could be friends. I have a feeling we're going to be neighbors." Helen's dark eyes slanted up to meet Cole's. "At least if Cole gets his way."

Veronica felt color tinge her cheeks, but she gave no other indication of the thrill of hope that surged inside her, showering her heart with joy.

"I'll call you tomorrow, Helen," Cole said to his sister-in-law. "Either that or I'll see you here at the hospital. Thanks again."

Cole and Veronica walked the rest of the way to his truck in silence. The sun had gone down, the dark-blue sky overhead deepening rapidly to diamond-studded blackness.

The ride home was quiet, as if both were too preoccupied with thoughts that couldn't be discussed yet. But when Cole pulled off the highway onto the ranch road, he took the left fork that led north of the house and deep into the rolling grazing land that stretched for miles beneath the night sky. He braked the truck to a halt on the crest of a hill and switched off the engine.

They sat in silence several moments, Cole's wrists draped over the top of the steering wheel as he stared into the darkness. Uncertain, Veronica tried to avoid the feeling that the next minute would be the most important of her life.

Sensing Cole was about to speak, she glanced in his direction. He leaned back, pulling his wrists from the steering wheel, and removed his Stetson. Lean tanned fingers pinched the crease of the hat as he looked down at it thoughtfully. Then he hung it on the rifle rack behind his head and turned to her, the lights from the dash illuminating the gentle loving look on his face and highlighting the vulnerability on hers.

Cole shook his head, his mouth tightening. "I'm sorry, Veronica. You deserve a more romantic setting than this."

Veronica's heart seemed to slam against her breastbone. Cole turned toward her fully, reaching to pull her into his arms. Veronica's hands slipped around his neck as his lips swooped down and took hers. When he deepened the kiss, Veronica felt the heated languor spread until she was thrall to the sensations his lips called forth.

"I love you, Veronica," Cole rasped. "And I'm going to be a miserable man if all you can say this time is that you 'care' for me." He didn't give her a chance to speak before his lips met hers with renewed vigor, releasing her mouth only when she was breathing as unsteadily as he. "Well?"

"Are you certain you want my love?" Veronica stalled, and Cole pressed a tender kiss on her mouth.

"You're scared to admit it, aren't you?" he asked, his eyes narrowing perceptively. "But you aren't a sixteen-year-old child experiencing her first crush, Ronnie. You're a woman," Cole said, then waited for her to speak.

"I love you, Cole," she finally whispered. "I loved you eight years ago, but what I felt at sixteen was only a childish version of what I feel now." Veronica turned her face slightly, deflecting another of Cole's kisses as she released a nervous breath. "I don't think you're going to be able to get rid of me very easily. I'm afraid I love you too much to leave you now."

Cole chuckled at Veronica's confession and she watched him almost worriedly.

"That's awfully damned convenient, Ronnie," he growled, "because once we stand up before the preacher, you're stuck with me for life, for better or worse, in sickness and in health. And I'm not some faint-hearted pantywaist who's going to take back my vow or break it over every little thing that comes along." Cole's expression relaxed. "So unless you're planning to marry me and stay married, you'd be wise to choose your next words with care."

"Wait, Cole." Veronica pressed her fingers gently over his mouth, her eyes glazing when Cole took a fingertip between his teeth and wrapped his lips seductively around it. Veronica stared, mesmerized by the sight, paralyzed by the molten pleasure that radiated in wave after delicious wave through her slim body. "S-stop." Cole grinned at the small stutter, the satisfied look in his warm gaze telling her he enjoyed arousing her. "We need to...talk."

Veronica barely had enough sanity to get the words out before she dazedly wondered what there was left to say. Cole reached up and took her hand away, but not before he turned it over and placed a kiss in its sensitive palm. Rational thought returned in slow degrees as violet eyes stayed fixed to much darker blue ones.

"Will you marry me, Veronica?"

"Oh, Cole, I..." The joy she felt tumbled over her, sending her blood pulsing through her veins in a frenzied staccato of exhilaration. "I want to marry you very much," she said. "But what about Curtis?" She had been a reluctant stepchild too many times for her to be insensitive to the boy's feelings.

"Curtis is coming around, sweetheart. Now that we know the reason for your problems with him and got rid of the source, he'll accept you. There's no doubt in my mind that he'll come to love you like a mother." Cole pressed his forehead to hers, the tips of their noses touching.

"And that brings me to the next problem," she whispered, running a gentle hand along Cole's whisker-roughened cheek. "I'll never be able to replace Jackie." Veronica caught back a small sob, amazed at the heartache she felt at the forlorn words.

Cole's fingers threaded into her hair and tugged her head back as he brought his lips down forcefully on hers.

Veronica welcomed the ferocity of his mouth, opening her own to the onslaught, encouraging the raw passion of it as she combed her fingers into his hair, pressing him even closer. At last Cole withdrew, his fingers tightening in her hair to keep her mouth from reclaiming his. He saw the tears that glittered in the depths of her eyes.

"I stopped looking for a replacement for Jackie a long time ago," he told her. "And now that I've come to love you, Veronica, I know it's not only possible for that kind of love to happen twice—" Cole's husky voice dropped to a whisper "—but it can run deeper and sweeter the second time around."

Veronica was nearly overcome with emotion. Cole held her close again, the way he clung to her underscoring his every word, leaving her with no doubt about his love for her.

"If you'd rather have a more romantic setting for this marriage proposal, I'm willing to take you someplace else." Cole drew back, gazing down into the violet eyes that shimmered in the faint light from the dashboard. "Just as long as you say yes."

"I've already had all the romantic trappings," Veronica whispered. "And that's all they turned out to be—trappings. But you've provided the most romantic part of any marriage proposal—your love."

Veronica kissed him sweetly and said, "Yes. I'll marry you, Cole. But for nothing less than you threatened," she added, smiling happily. "For better or worse, in sickness and in health," she repeated, secure in the knowledge that whatever the future held for them, their vows of the heart were eternal.

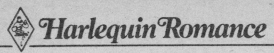 *Harlequin Romance*

Coming Next Month

Availabe in June wherever paperback books are sold, or
through Harlequin Reader Service.

In the U.S.
901 Fuhrmann Blvd.
P.O. Box 1397
Buffalo, N.Y. 14240-1397

In Canada
P.O. Box 2800, Postal Station
5170 Yonge Street
Willowdale, Ontario M2N 6J3

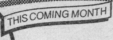

WORLDWIDE LIBRARY IS YOUR TICKET TO ROMANCE, ADVENTURE AND EXCITEMENT

Experience it all in these big, bold Bestsellers— Yours exclusively from WORLDWIDE LIBRARY WHILE QUANTITIES LAST

To receive these Bestsellers, complete the order form, detach and send together with your check or money order (include 75¢ postage and handling), payable to WORLDWIDE LIBRARY, to:

In the U.S.
WORLDWIDE LIBRARY
901 Fuhrmann Blvd.
Buffalo, N.Y. 14269

In Canada
WORLDWIDE LIBRARY
P.O. Box 2800, 5170 Yonge Street
Postal Station A, Willowdale, Ontario
M2N 6J3

Quant.	Title	Price
_____	WILD CONCERTO, Anne Mather	$2.95
_____	A VIOLATION, Charlotte Lamb	$3.50
_____	SECRETS, Sheila Holland	$3.50
_____	SWEET MEMORIES, LaVyrle Spencer	$3.50
_____	FLORA, Anne Weale	$3.50
_____	SUMMER'S AWAKENING, Anne Weale	$3.50
_____	FINGER PRINTS, Barbara Delinsky	$3.50
_____	DREAMWEAVER, Felicia Gallant/Rebecca Flanders	$3.50
_____	EYE OF THE STORM, Maura Seger	$3.50
_____	HIDDEN IN THE FLAME, Anne Mather	$3.50
_____	ECHO OF THUNDER, Maura Seger	$3.95
_____	DREAM OF DARKNESS, Jocelyn Haley	$3.95
_____		

YOUR ORDER TOTAL		$_____
New York and Arizona residents add appropriate sales tax		$_____
Postage and Handling		$___.75
I enclose		$_____

NAME _____

ADDRESS _____ APT.# _____

CITY _____

STATE/PROV. _____ ZIP/POSTAL CODE _____

WW-1-3

Can you keep a secret?

You can keep this one plus 4 free novels